CRACKERS

Insatiable Series
Book 2

Patrick Logan

Other Books by Patrick Logan

Insatiable Series
Skin (*Insatiable* Book 1)
The Crackers (*Insatiable* Book 2)
Flesh (*Insatiable* Book 3)

Stand-Alone Novels
Worm*
*Available January, 2016

Short Stories
System Update

Sign-up to my no spam newsletter at www.PTLBooks.com to receive *FREE* books!

The brain may be regarded as a kind of parasite of the organism, a pensioner, as it were, who dwells with the body.

- **Arthur Schopenhauer**

Prologue

SHERIFF PAUL WHITE HESITATED before opening the door. There was a strange energy in the air, a thickness to the atmosphere that made breathing a less than rudimentary task.

With the palm of his large black hand resting against the wooden door, he inhaled deeply, filling his considerable chest with vast quantities of air.

It's happening again.

The thought was odd, abstract, something that seemed wholly inappropriate at a time like this.

But the thought had been real, and it scared him.

The tingling in his fingers intensified as adrenaline, beginning as only a minor flush when he had first approached the room, started to diffuse throughout his entire body.

It had been six years since he had last felt this way — six whole years. An amazing feat considering that six years ago was the time that he had become the sheriff of Askergan County. And in all of that time since, learning the job on the fly, dealing with drunken idiots almost every weekend, and even handling a rash of break-ins, he had not felt a *rush* like this.

No, this *sensation* had been previously reserved for the blizzard and the horrible events that had taken place out at the Wharfburn Estate.

And now... *this.*

Another deep breath, and the sheriff finally pushed the door wide, trying not to let the fear that coursed through him show on his face.

"Good morning," he said curtly, observing the two figures sitting at the small metal table by the back of the square, ten-by-ten-foot room.

The man on the left, the one that looked to be in his late thirties or early-forties, had his arm wrapped around a boy of no more than sixteen years.

Greg and Kent Griddle, the sheriff affirmed based on the phone conversation that had taken place earlier.

"Morning, Sheriff," Greg replied.

The man went to stand, with the obvious intention of shaking hands, but the sheriff stopped him by reaching across the table and taking his hand before he had fully risen. The boy looked to be on the verge of a breakdown, and Paul thought it best if the boy's father kept his arm around him for comfort.

"Please, don't stand."

Even though the boy hadn't raised his head since the sheriff had entered, Sheriff White could tell that he had been crying. Even staring at the thick thatch of red hair that covered the top of his head, he could tell that the boy had shed many a tear this day; it was in the way his shoulders were slumped, how his hands were somehow loosely and firmly clasped at the same time, the way his breathing was hitched and uneven, and how the tops of his ears were a scarlet red.

"Greg Griddle," the boy's father said, drawing the sheriff's attention back. "We spoke on the phone earlier?"

The sheriff nodded.

"And this must be your son, Kent?" Paul asked, trying to elicit a response from the boy.

Kent failed to look up even at the mention of his name. Gregory turned to the boy and nudged him lightly with his elbow.

"Kent?"

When the boy still didn't respond, his father pulled his arm off of him with the intention of grabbing his shoulders in both hands. Maybe shake the life back into him.

Sheriff White quickly intervened by shaking his head.

Don't lose him, the sheriff tried to telepathically message Gregory. *I need to hear his story.*

Instead, the sheriff, still standing over the table, leaned in close and said, "Kent, I am here to help. You don't have to be scared anymore."

Paul wasn't sure if it was the third mention of the boy's name or the word *scared* that persuaded Kent to raise his head. When he finally looked up, he stared directly at the sheriff.

He was right, the boy had been crying, which was obvious by his raw, red-rimmed eyelids and by how the skin beneath his eyes was dry and chapped.

Kent opened his mouth to say something, but then closed it before words could escape him.

This time, Gregory spoke for him.

"We were on vacation, a fishing trip…"

The sheriff raised a hand and politely indicated that the man should stop talking. Then he turned back to Kent, who had reverted to staring at his clasped hands again.

"Thank you, Gregory, but I think I should hear this directly from Kent."

Gregory bit his lip and looked torn, and the sheriff quickly added, "If that's okay by you, of course."

The handsome man with light brown hair nodded slowly, silently offering the sheriff permission to continue.

Good.

Sheriff White needed to hear what happened from the boy, not through his proxy. And, as a minor, he was bound to the wishes of the man's father. Thankfully,

Gregory Griddle seemed like a reasonable man, a concerned father, who also sought the answers that niggled at the sheriff.

Leaning forward again, Sheriff White turned his attention back to the boy with the thick red hair.

"Kent?"

His tone was soft, inviting.

"First of all, Kent, I want to thank you for coming in here today. What you've done is very brave."

The boy's shoulders twitched—*shrugged, maybe?*—and the sheriff was encouraged to continue.

"And I want you to know that you aren't in trouble. Your father told me about the drinking, and I assure you that I don't care about that. And I also want you to know that you aren't a prisoner here; as far as I am concerned, you have done nothing wrong—you can leave at any time. But the more you tell me, the better our chances of finding your friend."

Kent visibly trembled at the word 'friend', yet his head remained bowed.

The sheriff turned quickly to the boy's father. The man was pale and had a vacant look in his eyes. Although Paul didn't have any children of his own, he thought he understood what the man was going through; it was plainly etched on his features. Gregory Griddle experienced his son's pain as if it were his own, and he felt responsible for it.

And that said nothing about how he had been the legal guardian of the other boy when he had gone missing.

For going on six years now, Paul White had been the sheriff of Askergan County, and he had been a deputy and officer in the same district for many years before that. And during all of that time, he had never heard a story like the one that Gregory Griddle had told him over the phone. Sure, Askergan had had its fair share of kids who ran away from home, trying to flee from an abusive father, or to shirk the often overwhelming responsibilities that came with puberty.

But nothing like this.

Sheriff Paul White had *never* heard a story like this… except for maybe once, when a similar tale had been woven by his then partner, Deputy Bradley Coggins.

Only once, after the blizzard.

And now *this* tale, with the Wharfburn Estate once again being the focal point.

An image of the massive house with the blackened doorway, reeking of burnt hair and charred wood, assaulted his senses with such ferocity that he nearly pulled away from the table and stood.

The sheriff fought the urge by leaning even more heavily on the table, feeling the cold metal dig into his meaty palms.

Focus.

"Kent, the more you can tell me about Tyler's disappearance, the better."

The mention of his friend's name finally encouraged the boy to lift his head again.

Fresh tears glistened on his round cheeks.

"You want to know about the house? About what I saw at the house?"

The boy's voice was hoarse and his expression blank. Paul was no psychologist, but to him it appeared as if the boy had already erected a wall in his mind—a wall to keep the past out, to protect himself against the horrors creeping on the other side.

It all seemed so familiar to the sheriff.

Another flash of the Wharfburn Estate, but he forced it away before it took hold.

Déjà vu.

"No, not the house, Kent," the sheriff said softly.

Ever since he had entered the room, he had been leaning on the table. But now that Kent looked like he was going to open up, he pulled a chair back from the table and slowly took a seat.

"Let's start at the beginning; tell me everything from even before you made it to the lake."

It would be hard, he knew, for the boy to recount the entire tale, especially if what Gregory had told him over the phone was anything like the real thing. But Paul knew a thing or two about interrogation, and even though this constituted more of an interview than anything else, the same rules applied: one, get the boy talking, try to grasp the boy's state of mind even prior to what had, or *allegedly* had, happened; and, two, pay close attention to the details of the story leading up to the event. It was his experience that when people made up stories—lied—the details flanking the event in question were unrehearsed, jagged and unkempt; this was a telltale sign that the story was a lie.

Kent nodded slowly and cleared his throat. The sheriff gently pushed a glass of water closer to the boy.

"Have a sip, take your time," he instructed.

It wasn't so much that the sheriff thought the boy was *lying*—shit, if this was all an act, give the kid an Oscar right now—but that maybe he had been confused.

Or *impaired*.

Kent Griddle took a sip of water and then placed it back on the table. His face lowered, his eyes finding whatever crisscrossing lines around his knuckles that he found so interesting.

Then he started to speak, and the sheriff shifted his weight from his palms to his forearms as he leaned in close and listened.

1.

"YOU ALMOST READY, CHAMP?"

Kent Griddle shoved his sleeping bag into the trunk with two hands, then watched as it slowly regained its shape. He stood there for a moment, scowling as the dark blue fabric continue to swell until there was more hanging out of the trunk than inside.

It's never going to fit.

"Almost," he replied, bringing a hand to the back of his head and tugging lightly at his short red hair.

It's never going to fit.

He stared at the obstinate sleeping bag, trying to will it inside the trunk. When that didn't work, he leaned around the side of the car.

"Dad?"

Gregory Griddle pulled his sunglasses down his

small nose and stared at his son through the side mirror. There was a glint of humor in his pale blue eyes.

"What's up?" he replied, running a hand through his medium-length light brown hair. When his hand fell away, his hair returned to exactly as it had been before: neatly parted on the left side, the thick, wavy top perfectly imperfect. He was a man of small features—a small nose, narrow chin, eyes that bordered on beady— but the collective sum was greater than its parts, creating a cohesive look that one wouldn't hesitate to refer to as attractive.

A bead of sweat formed on Kent's forehead, slowly becoming a drop before tracing a lazy line down the side of his cheek. He quickly wiped it away with the back of his hand.

"I don't—" he began, but the sleeping bag started to roll out of the trunk, and he quickly shoved it back in before it fell to the ground.

"God damn it," he muttered.

His father, still inspecting him through the side mirror, laughed.

"Don't sweat it, champ. Either put it in the trunk or toss it in the backseat—doesn't matter."

Kent scrunched his nose, the freckles that marked the bridge seeming to coalesce into a single frustrated smudge. But then his boyish features relaxed and he nodded, more to himself than to his father, and he pulled the dark blue sleeping bag out of the trunk. He gave the piece of plush fabric a look laced with venom, then glanced to the backseat, trying hard to make up his mind.

Backseat or trunk?

Gregory leaned further out the window, his armpit gripping the doorframe.

"Just make up your mind and let's get on the road!"

Kent glared at the sleeping bag clutched in his left hand. It looked like it would fit in the trunk, like it *should* fit; there was more than enough room for it squish on top of the cooler and tent.

Why don't you fit?

"Just throw it in the backseat! Why do you let these things get to you?"

Kent looked up quickly, worried that he would see annoyance plastered on his father's face. But Greg wasn't even looking at him; instead, he was staring off into the distance, thumping the pad of his thumb on the car door, his head bobbing to imaginary music.

Fucking sleeping bag.

Kent slammed the trunk closed and then tossed the sleeping bag in the backseat as he had been instructed.

"Relax," Gregory said, pushing his sunglasses back up his nose as his son opened the passenger door and climbed inside. "This is supposed to be fun," he added, reaching over and tousling Kent's short red hair. "Don't pout—makes you look like a baby."

Kent made a face.

"And don't sulk—makes you look like a girl."

Kent tried to direct his scowl at his father, but the

man's wide grin made it impossible for him to remain angry.

Greg laughed and turned the key.

The car cleared its throat and growled to life.

2.

THEY ARRIVED AT TYLER'S place less than an hour later, when the sun had nearly reached its apex, thick waves of unrelenting heat beating down on them. The interior of the car was sweltering and Kent's T-shirt clung uncomfortably to his body. Every few minutes, he peeled it away from his skin and let it go—it immediately snapped back, slapping his chest with an audible *thwack*.

"Kent, seriously, you need to relax. Smile a little."

Kent looked over at his father and gave him a terrible fake smile. Gregory shook his head, but his grin lingered.

A door slammed, drawing their attention to the apartment building in front of them. A slender boy with a shaved head stepped out from a dark brown door, one of countless identical doors marking every fifteen or so feet of the building. Like Kent, Tyler was sixteen years old, but unlike Kent, he looked much older. The boy had small, dark eyes, the color of which matched the stubble on his shaved head. Although his face was too narrow, his eyelids too thick—tired-looking—he might have been handsome had it not been for the thick pink scar that ran from the outside of his right eye to just below his lower lip. The boy raised a skinny arm that poked out from a sleeveless Metallica T-shirt that was two sizes too big. In the hand that remained at his side was a small overnight bag.

"Kent, you want the front seat or backseat?" Gregory asked, turning to face his son.

Kent turned toward the backseat. More than half of the seating area was taken up by three fishing rods and two tackleboxes. And then there was the damn sleeping bag.

He frowned.

"Well?" Gregory urged.

Kent looked back at Tyler, who was making his way slowly to the car. He was wearing a pair of jeans and un-tied high-tops—he was going to melt.

"Hey, hey!" Tyler hollered, his pace quickening. "My boy, Kent!"

Kent, still trying to decide which seat his father wanted him to take, opened the door and stepped out into the hot sun. He squinted in the bright light and brought the blade of his hand up to his forehead to shield his eyes.

"What's up?" he asked tentatively.

Gregory leaned out of his window.

"What's up, Tyler?" he shouted. "C'mon, get in! The fish will be all gone by the time we get there!"

Tyler smiled broadly, the scarred half of his face not rising quite as high as the other, making it look like the two halves didn't quite line up.

He bumped knuckles with Kent.

"I got shotgun in this sweet ride?" he asked, the grin still plastered on his face.

"Fine," Kent answered, and Tyler gave him a soft punch on the shoulder.

"'Atta boy."

As Kent pulled the front seat forward and climbed into the back, forcing the fishing paraphernalia to the other side to make enough room to sit, Tyler ran his thumb over the wheel well of the royal blue '72 Chevelle.

"Man, I love this car," he said in near awe. "Damn, Gregory, this is one sweet ride."

Gregory chuckled.

"Thanks, kid."

Tyler clicked the seat into place and climbed in, jamming the back of the seat into Kent's shins.

"That all you brought?" Kent's dad asked, indicating the small black bag in Tyler's hands with his chin.

"All I need," Tyler replied, pushing his seat back even further. "Only thing I'm missing is a cooler to keep all the fish I'm gonna catch in."

A smirk formed on Gregory's small mouth.

"Here, Kent," Tyler said, forcing the bag into the back. "Keep this back there, would ya? Need me some legroom."

When Kent made no move to take the bag, Tyler's smile grew and he tossed it on top of the fishing rods.

"Aw, don't pout, Kent," Tyler said. Even from behind, he could see his father's ears move ever so slightly; he was smiling too.

Kent's pout become a scowl as they pulled out of the parking lot and made their way back onto the road.

They had been driving in silence for fifteen minutes, content on listening to the air rushing through the open windows, when Tyler turned to the backseat.

"So Kent, why—?"

Gregory swore and slapped the side of his neck. When he pulled his hand away and inspected it, there was a thick black smear in the center of his palm.

"Damn parasites," Gregory muttered, smearing the deer fly's corpse on his jeans.

Tyler looked at the man and nodded in approval.

"Pretty impressive, Mr. Gr—"

Again Tyler was interrupted, but this time it was not a curse and a slap that drew his attention, but the sound of an explosion that ripped through the cabin.

3.

THE CAR SWERVED TO the left, but Gregory quickly righted the vehicle and pulled it onto the soft shoulder, all the while stomping madly with his left foot in an attempt to put out the flames.

"Kent!" he yelled, jamming the car into park even before it was fully stopped. "Grab the water!"

Kent shoved the sleeping bag to one side, rummaged through the fishing poles and tackleboxes, and grabbed the four-gallon plastic jug from behind his father's seat.

"Here!" he shouted, almost throwing the plastic bottle into the front seat. The smell of burning plastic filled his nose and mouth, and he coughed.

Tyler was already halfway out of the vehicle, but he paused to reach back inside and grab the bottle from Kent. He quickly unscrewed the cap and then passed it to Gregory, who was still stomping furiously, with both feet now, at the small flames that continued to lick the pedals from somewhere beneath the dash.

Kent pulled the door open and exited the car, taking big gulps of air, trying to force the caustic smell from his throat.

By the time he made it around the car to his father's side, the fire was already out. The three of them stood there by the side of the road, only a couple of feet from the car, their eyes fixed on the still bubbling driver side floor mat.

"Huh," Gregory grunted after nearly a minute of silence, his eyes locked on the warped plastic that slowly began to flatten as it cooled.

Another few moments passed, none of them sure what to say next; Gregory's grunt fairly accurately expressed their collective feelings. Clearly, they were all a little embarrassed at how they had overreacted to the small fire.

"What happened?" Tyler asked at long last as he jammed his hands into his jean pockets.

Gregory shrugged.

"Dunno."

"Electrical?"

"Probably the catalytic converter," Gregory offered, his tone strangely nonchalant. "Been having trouble with some gunk buildup in there lately."

Tyler nodded.

More silence.

As the caustic smoke cleared from the passenger seat, Kent stared intently into the car, attempting to assess the extent of the damage.

A melted floor mat, warped plastic on the inside of the door, and some of the underside of the driver's seat had turned black, the leather cracked and split; all in all, it really wasn't that serious.

"Well it sounded bad," he offered with a shrug.

A bead of sweat trickled down his temple, but when he went to brush it away, he missed and nearly poked himself in the eye with a trembling finger.

"I think it was the converter," Gregory repeated, more to himself this time than to either of the boys. He sighed, and then added, "Only one way to find out."

With that, Gregory reached into the car and pulled the hood release latch on the lefthand side of the steering wheel. Then he grabbed the nearly empty jug of water from the damp ground and brought it to his lips, gulping loudly. Water spilled down his chin, which he promptly wiped away with the back of his arm.

"Let's take a look."

*　　　*　　　*

Gregory had been right; it was the catalytic converter that had started the fire. Although he went to great lengths to explain what had happened, how it had become clogged, then how it must have burst a rivet and fuel had leaked onto the casing—blah, blah, blah—Kent blocked most of this out; unlike his father, he had little interest in cars, aside from their obvious convenience. Tyler, on the other hand, appeared rapt, hanging on his every word.

"Can we drive without it?" Kent asked hesitantly, unsure of whether or not this was a completely moronic question.

Gregory turned to face his son. Kent half expected to see one of his father's patented sidelong smirks—the infamous Griddle *'C'mon now'* expression—but instead, the man's handsome features were soft and almost flaccid.

"You ever been on a Harley?" he asked, scratching at the stubble on his cheek.

Kent made a face; of course he hadn't been on a bike—and his dad knew that.

"I have," Tyler answered.

Gregory nodded as if to say, *I knew you had,* and Kent's expression became a frown.

"Well, you're gonna experience what it sounds like, at least," Gregory finished.

The man let go of the hood and it closed loudly. As he made his way back to the open driver's side door, he traced a finger across the hood and over the front wheel well.

"And yes," he added, "we can drive without it."

4.

"YOU GOT WHAT I need, girl," Kent belted from the backseat. He had to nearly scream for his voice to be heard over the raw rumble of the engine. "Girl, you got what I need!"

Gregory bobbed his head with the tune, then ran the backs of his fingers up the air vent, making a *thrrup* sound. He followed this up by strumming his fingers on the dash: *brrd*.

"Yeah," Kent continued, "you got what I need, girl!"

Thrrup, brrd brrd brrd.

The sounds melted into the engine's barks, generating an oddly robotic cacophony.

Tyler laughed and shook his head.

"You guys don't even know the words!"

Kent responded by singing the next verse even

louder.

When the song finally ended, Tyler shook his head again and turned his sweat-covered face to the backseat.

"You guys," he said, then mouthed *are fucked* to his friend.

Now it was Kent's turn to laugh.

"C'mon, Tyler, you can't tell me you don't like that tune," Gregory said.

Tyler turned back to the front seat.

"No way."

Gregory turned to him, eyeing his Metallica T-shirt.

"What, only heavy metal for you?" Gregory asked with a smirk.

"Yeah."

"I bet you don't even know any of their songs."

"Who? Metallica?"

Gregory nodded.

"Sure do! Ride the Lightning, Master of Puppets—" Gregory didn't let him finish.

"You are too young to know Metallica."

Tyler rolled his eyes.

"You know, when I was your age, I used to go to all the Metallica concerts—back before they started to go all pop."

Tyler scoffed.

"*Pop*? You were just singing Britney Spears!" he accused.

Kent laughed again.

"Not Britney Spears," Gregory corrected the boy.

"Whatever, same shit."

"Gotta like 'em all," Gregory added, as he reached forward and turned down the radio.

They drove without speaking for the next little while, their molars rattling from the engine noise. Eventually, the road before them transitioned from a deep black tarmac to a faded grey, then to one consisting of more dirt and rocks than asphalt.

Kent continued to pull the shirt away from his body every few minutes, now more in an effort to cool himself than to alleviate the uncomfortable feeling of it clinging to his body. After Gregory had removed the catalytic converter, not only did the car sound like a 747 taking off, but for some reason the AC unit had stopped working as well; the only thing coming out of the air vents were small bursts of lukewarm air, like the final gasps of a wheezing old man.

"Engine is getting too hot," Greg said, more to himself than to anyone else. His eyes flicked to the temperature gauge on the dash, watching as the needle trembled closer to the orange 'H' than he felt comfortable.

"Hey, Kent, you okay back there? Cool enough for you?"

Kent wiped the sweat from his brow and plucked at his T-shirt again.

"Want the windows open, or is the AC enough?"

AC? What AC?

The reflective lenses of his dad's sunglasses flicked up to the rearview mirror.

"Kent?"

But before Kent had an opportunity to answer, Tyler cut in.

"Let's get some air circulating through this beast."

"Good idea," Gregory replied, rolling down his window. "Don't want it to overheat."

Opening the windows didn't help much; the air that blasted Kent in the face was hot and laced with the smell of sweat from the car's front seat passengers. To make it worse, the noisy wind added to the obnoxious rumbling from the engine, making it difficult for him to hear any of the conversation up front. He leaned forward, pressing his cheek against the side of Tyler's hot leather seat, trying to remain part of the conversation.

"Speaking of music, did you bring your guitar, Mr. Griddle?"

Gregory smiled.

"You bet I did."

"Awesome."

Tyler reached forward and turned the radio back up, just as the song ended and the DJ's voice broke the airwaves.

"And now for your throwback tune at noon," the DJ said. "We have something special for you today… something from way, waaaaay back. A little—*boom boom boom*—something heavy for you on this sweltering summer day; a little Metallica."

Tyler's eyes went wide.

"Ah snap!" he exclaimed. "What are the odds?"

Gregory laughed and nodded his head. Then he ran his fingers up the air vent again.

Thrrup, brrd brrd brrd.

5.

THE SUN WAS STILL high in the sky and the temperature hovering around one hundred when they finally
reached the campsite.

Gregory turned off the car—which sighed and then
shuddered with the relief of having its boiling engine
shut down—and peeled himself off the leather seat. Tyler groaned and stretched his legs.

"You've got a great car, Mr. Griddle, but—no offense—your AC *suckkkks.*"

"What can I say? It's an oldie but a goody—just like
Metallica."

Tyler waved a hand in front of his face.

"Stinks, too," he added.

Tyler exited the car and then yanked the seat forward.
It took Kent four tries before he managed to haul himself

out.

The three of them stood beside the '72 Chevelle for a few moments, stretching away the stiffness that had built up over the long, hot ride. Although the sun continued to beat down on them relentlessly, the fresh air blowing off the lake behind them offered a minor reprieve from the sweltering interior of the classic car.

Kent stared at the dark wisps of smoke coming from somewhere beneath the car, and a caustic smell wafted up to him, but neither Gregory nor Tyler seemed alarmed. Kent shrugged and took a step backward, trying to maximize his exposure to the lake breeze at his back.

"All right, boys, you unload while I go see where the rest of them are."

Gregory turned to Kent and his son nodded.

"Sure," Kent replied, wiping sweat from his forehead and plucking at his shirt again. The white fabric was almost completely grey now, and it hugged his body like a second skin.

"Get your game faces on, boys, the fish are waiting."

*   *   *

"Hey, check this out," Tyler said, reaching into his small bag.

The boy was sprawled out on the cool grass while Kent was sitting defiantly on his obstinate sleeping bag. The large oak tree that arced over their heads offered them some relief from the sun, but even with the lake breeze, the air was still hot and stifling. Tyler pulled himself to a seated position and withdrew a clear glass bottle out of his bag.

Kent eyed the bottle suspiciously.

"Vodka," Tyler informed him, smiling broadly.

He passed the bottle to Kent. Then he brought his cigarette to his lips and took another drag.

Kent held the bottle up to the sun.

"It's half full," he said as he sloshed the liquid from side to side.

Tyler smiled again. The scar on his cheek was slick and glistening with sweat, giving him a slightly sinister appearance.

"I know," he chuckled, "took it from my ma."

Kent raised an eyebrow.

"She's not gonna notice?"

"Fuck no." He took another drag. "She's usually so hopped up on pain pills that I doubt she'll even notice I'm gone."

Kent smiled.

"Sweet."

"Boys? You still alive back there?"

It was Gregory.

"Shit."

Kent frantically passed the bottle back to Tyler, who tucked it into his bag. He quickly zipped the bag closed, then flicked his cigarette away.

"Back here, Dad," Kent shouted, pulling himself to

his feet.

Gregory walked toward them, followed by a tall, thin man wearing a Tilley hat pulled low and sporting a beige fishing vest. He looked like a poor man's *Italo Labignan*. Picking up the rear was a young, muscular boy wearing a matching Tilley hat.

"Sergio!" Kent and Tyler exclaimed in unison.

"Yeah, buddy!"

Sergio hurried over to his friends and bumped fists with Kent.

"'Bout time you got here," Sergio said with a smile. "What's up, Tyler?"

"Chillin'."

"Welcome, boys!" Sergio's father shouted enthusiastically.

Now safely protected from the hot sun by the large oak tree, the man reached up and used two thin fingers to push the Tilley hat back from his eyes.

"Hey, Mr. Salvados," Kent replied.

Nick Salvados raised his prominent nose to the sky and sniffed loudly. Then he turned his gaze to the dark blue '72 Chevelle.

"What happened to your baby?" he asked.

Gregory's face suddenly grew stern.

"Catalytic converter popped," he said, but then his smile returned. "Had a nice little foot-warming effect."

Gregory raised his leg, showing off the undulating rubber sole that had been warped from the fire.

Nick smiled.

"Excitement already, eh, boys?"

Tyler nodded.

"No shortage of excitement on this trip, that's for sure," the boy said with a grin.

"She'll be fine," Gregory added, slapping Nick on the back. "And look who else I found!" he exclaimed, stepping around Nick.

On cue, a portly kid of no more than fifteen stepped out from behind Nick Salvados' shadow. He was pudgy around the middle, with a round face to match. The boy's blond hair was trimmed straight across his bangs, and sweat glued the thin strands to his forehead like the tines of a garden rake. Although he had only appeared a few seconds ago, he had already twice pulled at his jean shorts and tight polo shirt. In a word, the boy looked uncomfortable, a fact that was reflected in his awkward smirk.

"Fucking Baird," Tyler whispered out of the corner of his mouth, averting his eyes.

Although he had barely mouthed the words, evidently they were just loud enough for Gregory to hear. Kent's dad turned sideways so that he was only visible to Sergio, Kent, and Tyler, and he whispered back, "Be nice."

Tyler rolled his eyes but said nothing.

Baird's father came next, a striking contrast to his son: tall and muscular, with a shock of dark brown hair. He had the beginnings of a beard, a five o'clock shadow that had appropriately appeared at just about five o'clock.

"And this is Baird's dad, Reggie," Gregory continued. Tyler couldn't hold back his shock.

"You have to be kidding me," he muttered. Then he turned to Kent, eyebrows raised. "Fucking mailman?" he whispered, this time making sure that only Kent could hear.

Kent laughed, and his father, although he couldn't have possibly overheard this time, gave him a stern look.

Baird's father offered his son an encouraging push on the small of his back, and the chubby kid stumbled forward a few steps.

"Go on," Reggie urged.

"Hey, guys," Baird finally mumbled, eyes downcast.

It was Sergio who answered.

"'Sup, Baird."

Gregory Griddle, face still stern, gave his son an aggressive nod, and Kent reluctantly spoke up.

"'Sup."

Tyler followed next with something that might have been "Hello", or could have just as easily been "Fuck you".

Kent watched as Sergio's dad gave Reggie a big hug, and his own father followed suit.

"Nice to see you, big fella," Gregory said with a smile. "You ready to catch some Muskies?"

"Oh yeah."

"Boat ready?"

Nick pushed his Tilley hat further up his forehead, revealing a dark, almost black widow's peak, and shook his head.

"Can't go out tonight, unfortunately—owner said there was a problem with the boat's starter."

Gregory frowned.

"Said it's gonna be up and running in the morning, though. Mechanic is going get out here in an hour or so—make sure we can go bright and early in the AM."

Reggie checked his watch quickly.

"Almost five thirty anyway," he informed the group. "All the fish are sleeping by now, right, Baird?"

Baird looked shocked that he was called upon, and he stopped toe-digging and looked up. Tyler rolled his eyes so dramatically that Kent could have sworn he heard his ocular muscles strain.

"C'mon, Baird, tell the boys what you told me about fish in the car on the way up."

Baird hesitated, but after another encouraging nod from his father he finally spoke up. His voice didn't seem to match his round body—it was high and tight, as if he were eleven and not fifteen.

"Fish are cold-blooded," he said slowly, "meaning that they don't regulate their body temperature like mammals."

When Baird noticed that all eyes were on him, his gaze returned to the bare earth by his feet.

"So when the sun is out," he continued, "they like to

stick to the shade—deep in the weeds. Especially Muskies, because they are such large fish. Very difficult to
get them to bite during the day; better off in the even-
ing—or, better still, in the morning."

"See?" Reggie smiled, patting his son on the back.
"Morning is better anyway."

"Morning is better," Baird confirmed.

"Well, then," Gregory said, "Baird, why don't you
help the boys bring our gear up to the campsite while
we go check us in?"

When Baird failed to respond, Reggie gave his son another friendly shove. .

"Go on, Baird. Go help your friends."

*　　*　　*

"Can't you carry anything else?" Tyler grumbled.

"I'm carrying as much as I can," Baird huffed.

Kent looked over at him. The chubby boy was clutching a fishing pole in each hand, trying desperately to
balance them so that the tips didn't stick in the dirt. Tyler, on the other hand, had his black bag over one shoulder and was trying to wrap his arms around Kent's obstinate sleeping bag. Sergio was also carrying his fair
share: a tacklebox in each hand, and a tent draped across
both arms. As Kent watched, Tyler's stretched fingers finally managed to grasp the backside of the sleeping bag,
and he squeezed it to his chest and stood.

"You're fucking cold-blooded," Tyler grumbled.

"Maybe that's why your arms are so fucking weak."

"That doesn't even make sense," Baird corrected him.

"I'm a mamm—"

"Maybe that's why your dick is so small, too."

Sergio laughed, and Kent couldn't help the smile that crossed his lips. Tyler's inane comments always had a way of getting to him, which was probably why they were such good friends despite their glaring differences.

One of the fishing poles in Baird's hands snagged in the dirt and he stumbled, barely catching himself before falling.

"I don't think—"

Kent shifted the two bags that crisscrossed his sweat-soaked shirt.

"Let's just get the stuff to the campsite, okay?"

6.

THE CAMPFIRE SHONE BRIGHTLY, illuminating the otherwise dark night. Thick, flat clouds had rolled in after dinner, blanketing the campers and the moon in a mild chill.

Kent rolled his marshmallow slowly over the open flame, relishing at how perfectly brown and bubbly the sugary outer layer had become.

Nearly perfect.

He took a break from admiring his own roasted marshmallow and turned to Baird.

What the fuck?

Not only had Baird lit his entire marshmallow on fire, but his stick was also alight.

"Jesus," Baird muttered, shaking his stick back and forth. Bits of flaming marshmallow whipped about the campfire like confetti.

"Baird!" Reggie shouted, reaching to stop his son, while at the same time leaning away from him in an attempt to avoid being splattered by the scalding sugar shower.

Baird seemed not to notice, too obviously worried about losing one of his last marshmallows, and continued to shake the stick violently. Thankfully, for the sake of their skin, the charade didn't last long as the boy's stick suddenly broke and the flaming half, with the marshmallow still burning like a medieval torch, fell into the fire.

Baird whined.

"Baird, why don't you look at what how Kent is doing it?"

Kent rolled his eyes. It was like watching a three-year-old frustrated with a one-thousand-piece puzzle; no matter how hard they tried, the patience or mental capacity eluded them.

Reggie reached into the bag of marshmallows at his side; it was nearly empty. Despite having already polished off at least a dozen by himself, Baird was no better at toasting them now than he had been with his first.

Reggie handed his son a marshmallow and again indicated to Kent with his chin. Kent nodded proudly and rolled his marshmallow a third time, the now crispy exterior a good three feet above the furthest licks of the fire.

"Take your time, son."

Baird snatched the raw marshmallow greedily and then looked around for a replacement stick.

Sergio, who for some reason hated marshmallows— *who hates marshmallows?*—was sitting on a log with his father across from both Kent and his dad. All of them save Tyler were wearing long-sleeved shirts and jeans.

"I thought it was supposed to be warm this weekend. It's the dead of summer," Nick Salvados muttered, rubbing his thighs.

Gregory Griddle looked at his friend.

"It *was* warm," he said. "It was blisteringly hot—so hot that it melted my shoes."

"Well it's downright freezing out here now."

"Bah, it's not that bad," Gregory replied, reaching into his own bag for another marshmallow. "Right, son?"

Kent didn't notice anything going on around him; he was completely transfixed on his marshmallow. *Now* it was perfect: the surface was completely brown, just dark enough to form a crust, some charred sugar to crack with his teeth, but with an interior that was undoubtedly warm and sticky.

"Kent? Kent, I'm talking to you."

A small bubble of caramelized sugar rose on the surface before deflating slowly.

Someone suddenly grabbed his roasting stick partway between his hand and the perfect gem of a marshmallow.

"Yeah, Kent," Tyler said, wrenching the stick from

Kent's grasp. "Your dad is talking to you."

"Hey!" Kent cried, but it was too late.

In one smooth motion, Tyler reached down, grabbed the still bubbling marshmallow, and shoved it into his gaping mouth.

"Tyler, what the—?" Kent stopped himself before dropping the F-bomb.

Even though his mouth must have been on fire, his upper pallet just screaming from the intense heat, Tyler smiled. He looked eerie, the campfire light illuminating his entire face save the scar; it looked like his face was split in two.

"Tyler! That was—"

"Here, Kent," Gregory said calmly, and then passed his son the half-empty bag of marshmallows.

Kent, still leering at Tyler, missed the bag, and five or six of the white cylinders spilled onto the ground. Baird, who was searching desperately for a new roasting stick, heard the bag fall and immediately chimed in.

"Guys! Don't waste any—we don't have many more left!" He was still clutching the half-full bag that his dad had given him moments ago.

Sergio chuckled, and even Sergio's dad, not known for being the most humorous of men, lit up with a smile.

"You ass—" Kent began, his face beginning to redden, but Gregory spoke up in a tone that suggested he should drop it.

"Give it up, guys," he said.

Kent continued to glare at Tyler, but said nothing

more.

You asshole!

"No sticks!" Baird said, from somewhere in the brush behind them.

"Let's try something else, shall we?" Gregory offered, reaching behind the log and pulling out his acoustic guitar.

"Yeah, let's," Tyler said eagerly. He smiled, a half-hearted, pained expression, no doubt a reflection of his burning mouth.

Good. Serves you right.

Kent knew that in the morning the inside Tyler's mouth would peel away like a layer of film on a tub of gravy left in the fridge overnight, and this thought offered him a modicum of satisfaction.

Serves you right.

To facilitate an end to the whole fiasco, Gregory strummed his guitar.

"What do you guy want to hear?"

"Metallica," Tyler answered predictably. He clucked his tongue in an attempt to remove the thick layer of sugar that clung to the roof of his mouth.

"Yeah," Sergio said.

Gregory rolled his eyes.

He began plucking away at the strings. "How about this one?"

It only took a couple of chords before both Kent and Tyler recognized the tune. But Kent, still furious with Tyler, continued to sulk, even as his father broke into song.

"You got what I *need*."

Now it was Tyler's turn to scowl.

"Terrible song," Sergio's father muttered, which just made Greg sing louder.

"I know, right?" Tyler said.

Reggie buried his face in his hands, while Baird looked on as if he had never heard the tune before. The chubby boy took a break from scrounging around the campfire for a roasting stick and stared at Gregory's fingers as they moved hypnotically across the strings. Although it was clear from his expression that he had no idea what the song was, his lips moved slightly as if he were looking for a place to join in.

"You got what I need," Gregory sang. "Come on, everyone, join in!"

Reggie reluctantly pulled his face out of his hands and grumbled a few lines. Nick joined in next, and Sergio hummed along with his father. Tyler resisted, his thin lips tightly pressed together. Even Baird started to sing now, though it was clear that he didn't know the words. Finally, when he could resist no longer, Kent found himself muttering the words to the catchy tune.

The song ended in a loud cacophony that echoed off the trees surrounding the campsite. As the laughter erupted, even Tyler couldn't keep the scowl etched on his face, and he eventually joined in as well.

Although Greg had only played one song, it had been

a long drive and it seemed best that they retire on a joyous note.

"That's it," Gregory exclaimed with a laugh. "I'm done!"

As if to back up his words, he reached behind the log on which he sat and grabbed his guitar case.

"No Metallica?" Tyler asked, raising his eyebrows.

"Not tonight, Tyler. Tomorrow night—I promise."

Tyler nodded. Despite his obvious detestation of the song, he too was wrapped up in the collective joviality.

As Gregory put his guitar back into his case and the rest of the group began collecting their things, Baird just stood there looking lost.

"One more marshmallow?" he asked.

Reggie answered immediately.

"No, son, time for bed."

Baird nodded slowly, his expression grim.

"Tyler, why don't you help me put out this fire?" Gregory asked. "Oh, and maybe it will be fun for you boys to share a tent?"

Kent's eyes flipped up and he looked at his father—he was always the one his dad asked to help put out the campfire.

Gregory looked away and continued hurriedly.

"Kent, you stay with Baird and—"

"I'll stay with Sergio," Tyler said quickly. It was clear that Gregory wanted Tyler to join Kent and Baird, but seeing the crooked smile on Tyler's face, he relented and nodded slowly.

"I guess that means I'm with you two goons," Gregory said, indicating Reggie and Nick with the head of his guitar just before he closed the case.

"Gonna be a tight fit," Reggie noted, but despite his comment, he seemed game.

"Go get some water from the lake, Tyler," Gregory repeated. "We better put out this pathetic excuse for a bonfire."

*   *   *

Kent was alone in his tent when someone scratched at the fabric.

"Yeah?"

"It's me," Gregory said softly. "Can I come in?"

"Sure."

The tent unzipped and his father's face filled the opening, his blue eyes scanning the interior of the tent.

"Where's Baird?"

"Brushing his teeth," Kent answered curtly.

His dad nodded, and then eased his body partway into the tent.

"Listen," he began in a soft voice, "I want to talk to you about something."

Kent folded his sleeping bag under his arms and stared at his father. Although he was still annoyed by the way his dad had failed to back him up when Tyler had grabbed his marshmallow—his absolutely perfectly roasted marshmallow—and how he had asked Tyler to help him put out the fire, Gregory Griddle wasn't a particularly emotional man, and his unexpectedly somber tone broke down Kent's guard.

"Listen, you know why I'm so nice to your friend Tyler, don't you?"

Kent nodded slowly, confirming the man's words without really understanding them.

Tyler? Why does he want to talk about Tyler?

Greg lowered his eyes for a moment, and he picked at the zipper on Kent's sleeping bag. A second later, he looked up again and stared directly into his son's eyes before continuing.

"I knew his father once," Gregory began. "He was—well, he was a troubled boy who grew into a troubled man."

Kent thought he saw his dad shudder. Gregory looked away again, this time as if he were remembering something, his attention drawn to the crisscrossing poles at the apex of the tent.

"And his mother, well—you know his mother; she has some problems, too."

This time, Kent nodded more obviously. Tyler wasn't one to have company often, but he had been to his friend's house a few times after they had been out drinking and he didn't want to come home and risk getting caught by his own family. Although they had gone through extensive measures to sneak inside without being noticed—special ops-type measures—their efforts had been unnecessary; Tyler's mom was always passed out on the couch with the TV blaring. And each time, there had been a half-empty bottle of vodka on the coffee table, sitting beside a matching half-empty jar of pills. Indeed, Mrs. Wandry had some problems as well.

"Yeah," Kent said softly.

"So I just—I just want to give the kid a chance. An outlet, somewhere he can feel safe and welcome, you know? And I think... I think he needs some structure, rules to keep him straight. Do you get what I'm saying?"

Kent nodded again. The fact was, he thought he knew where his father was coming from, and in some weird way he was proud of him for expressing himself so openly. Still, it hurt that one of his father's rare emotional moments had nothing to do with him.

"I get it, Dad," he replied softly.

Any seriousness in Gregory's face vanished, and was immediately replaced by one of his famous side-mouth grins.

"Good. And you know that you are—" He reached into the tent to tousle Kent's hair, but Kent lay down quickly and the man's arm fell short.

Gregory's smile grew.

"Well," he laughed, "you know you're my champ, right?"

Kent nodded again.

"Hey, listen, you want to stay in this tent with Baird, or do you want to switch with Tyler or Sergio?"

Kent stared at his dad. It was clear that the man wanted to do right by him, to include him in some of the decisions, but he was torn. Gregory had already divvied up the sleeping arrangements, and besides, who was to say that Tyler and Sergio weren't already asleep?

It was the sleeping bag fiasco all over again—trunk or backseat?

Make up your damn mind, Kent.

"Kent?" His father looked on.

Just as Kent opened his mouth to answer, someone stumbled outside the tent, and Gregory leaned his head out.

"Baird's back," his dad said, tapping Kent's knee through his sleeping bag.

That was it; the decision had been made—and once again, Kent hadn't made it.

"Goodnight, champ."

Kent nodded.

"'Night, Dad."

"Sleep well, boys," Gregory said to them both as he pulled himself out of the tent.

*   *   *

Kent lay awake long after his father had left. It was Baird: the boy's snoring was a terrible assault of wet, bubbling pops followed by breathless gasps.

Jesus Christ.

Twice, he had shaken the boy awake to get him to roll over in an attempt to put an end to the obnoxious noise. And while this worked for a minute or two, just when

Kent's eyelids started to droop, the snoring would start again and he would be wide awake. How he regretted not telling his father that he wanted to sleep with Tyler, Sergio, or the goddamn boogeyman instead of sleeping with Baird.

Goddamn it, why can't you just make up your mind?

He was about to wake Baird again, but then he heard a noise outside the tent and he lay there, trying to pick out the sound amidst the noise from the slumbering manatee beside him. His heart was racing.

Then he heard what sounded like a stumble, followed by a curse, and his heartrate returned to normal; it was only Tyler.

Baird snorted loudly and his eyes popped open.

"What? What happened?" he practically shouted, the boy's retainer making the words nearly unintelligible.

The tent suddenly unzipped and Tyler poked his head in.

"Shut the fuck up, Baird," he said, then winced and sat inside their tent, rubbing his foot. "Stubbed my goddamned toe."

"What's up, Tyler?" Kent asked, pulling himself onto his elbows.

Tyler smiled.

"Looky looky what I got!" he exclaimed, his smile spreading. He abandoned rubbing his foot and pulled the half-empty bottle of vodka into the tent.

"What is that?" Baird asked, his eyes wide.

Tyler made a face at the sounds that came out of the

boy's retainer-filled mouth and ignored him.

"How 'bout a nightcap, then we go exploring?"

He sloshed the liquid provocatively in the bottle as he spoke.

Kent was torn—he wasn't really that tired, and midnight exploring was a prospect he had been excited about prior to leaving for the trip. On the other hand, his dad would be pissed if he found out they'd left the tent to go wandering around in the dark.

One look at Tyler's face and he knew that *he* would be pissed if they *didn't* go.

"Well?" Tyler asked, unscrewing the top of the bottle. "Make up your mind, Kent."

Doomed if you do, doomed if you don't.

Thankfully, Baird spoke up before things got awkward.

"I don't think we should go tonight."

Tyler's smile faded.

"I think—" Kent started, but Tyler cut him off.

"Fine," he said petulantly before taking a swig from the bottle. Despite his attempts at looking tough, he grimaced as he swallowed. "I didn't want to go tonight, anyway."

"But—but, for sure I'm in tomorrow night," Kent said quickly.

When Tyler's scowl remained, he added, "For sure. I promise."

"Whatever."

Tyler screwed the cap back on and then turned to

Baird, who was still staring, wide-eyed. The index finger of the hand grasping the neck of the vodka bottle shot out like an arrow.

"Baird, shut the fuck up about this. If you tell your dad, I'll kill you."

Baird reached into his mouth and pulled out the retainer, thick gobs of saliva clinging to the pink-and-silver orthodontic.

"I wasn't going—"

"Shut up and don't piss the bed."

Tyler left without another word, leaving the tent door flapping open behind him.

Kent frowned and leaned forward. He had zipped the tent halfway when Baird placed a hand on his shoulder.

"Wait," he said in his high-pitched voice, "I have to pee."

7.

Kent wasn't sure why he had awoken.

During his slumber, his sleeping bag had worked its way up over his mouth, and his breathing had made the top few inches of the fabric moist with condensation.

But his ears had been out, and he could have sworn something, or someone, had jarred him awake.

He pulled the sleeping bag down and perked his ears.

There was Baird's breathing, the rhythmic sound of the boy's snoring mixed with his retainer rattling about in his slobbery mouth like loose train tracks. But that collective cacophony had been present all night—ever since the boy's eyes had fallen shut; *immediately* after they had closed.

No, there had been something else. Otherwise, the heavy sleeper that he was, he would not have awoken.

Kent concentrated hard, trying his best to push Baird's snores into the background.

He picked up the typical campground noises: lapping water, leaves brushing the wind, and the hissing of various insects and creatures that were best left undiscovered.

But there was something else, too.

Kent waited, and a few seconds later he heard it again: a moan. Underlying all of the other sounds was the unmistakable sound of a human moan.

Kent's breath caught in his throat, and his wide eyes darted over to Baird. The boy, lying flat on his back, half out of his sleeping bag, arms splayed at his sides, hadn't moved.

He listened harder, his ears getting hot either from the effort or from the adrenaline that suddenly surged through his blood.

There.

Beneath the sounds of the forest was the deep rumble of a moan from somewhere outside his tent.

Kent's first instinct was just to go back to sleep, to close his eyes and allow the sweet, comforting blanket of slumber to once again envelope his senses. But when the moan came a third time, he found himself unable to ignore it. His heart racing now, he pulled the sleeping bag down further and sat up.

As was his habit, he made a deal with himself: if he heard the sound again before he could count to ten in his head, he would go investigate. If not, he would ignore it the best he could and go back to sleep... if sleep were at all possible.

One, two, three, four.

Kent took a deep breath and closed his eyes tightly.

Fivesixseveneightnine—

On *ten* he heard it again, only this time it wasn't just a moan. This time, the moan was accompanied by a word.

"Come."

For some reason, the word, so benign on its own, held more weight than it should have and a shudder ran wracked his entire body. A third glance over at Baird— *please be awake, please be awake*—revealed that the boy was still locked in his Christ-like pose, snoring away. There would be no support from him this night.

Against his better judgement, but unwilling to cheat himself, Kent pulled his legs from the sleeping bag and carefully unzipped the tent.

It was unexpectedly cold outside, and the tremor that had previously flowed through him transitioned into a full-out shiver. Even more unexpected was that without Baird's underlying retainer chatter, the other sounds seemed to vanish as well, until the forest was almost completely silent.

Except for the moan, of course; that was still there.

Without a flashlight, Kent had to resort to using moonlight as his only source of illumination. Luckily the lake was like a sheet of glass, and the moon's rays re-

flected off of it like a beacon. He subconsciously followed the path to the lake, and this led him directly to
the source of the moan.

Tyler, still fully dressed save his running shoes, was
sitting alone on a log near the extinguished fire that they
had all gathered around a few hours ago.

If he hadn't already been shaking, the sight of his
friends hunched formed staring into nothingness would
have certainly sent a chill up Kent's spine.

"Tyler?" he whispered, trying his best not to startle
the boy. It was all he could do to get the words out without his teeth chattering.

Tyler sat with his back to him, his shoulders hunched,
elbows firmly pressed against his thighs. As Kent continued to approach, the boy slowly raised his head. When
he was within a few feet of the fire pit, Tyler slowly
turned and looked directly at him.

The moonlight reflected off his scar, giving his entire
face an eerie appearance. But this wasn't what stopped
Kent's advance short.

It was his eyes: despite the fact that the boy's eyes
were wide, they were glassy and vacant—empty. It
looked like he was still asleep, but his lips were moving
and as Kent watched, slurred words fell from his mouth.

"It wants us to *come*," the boy said, his words but a
hushed, wet whisper. "It wants us to go to it, *needs* us to
go to it."

Kent's heart, which was already racing, kicked into
overtime and he felt his fingertips begin to tingle.

It *wants us to come?*

As if Tyler had read his thoughts, the boy nodded loosely.

"It wants us to *come*," he repeated.

Kent swallowed hard.

"What wants us to come, Tyler?" The words were choked, as if his throat had constricted to the width of a straw. "Who, Tyler?"

Instead of answering, Tyler's eyes slowly rolled back into his head. A moment later, the shivering that affected Kent seemed to transfer to his friend.

Fearing that Tyler was about to convulse, Kent forced his own fear away and rushed to the boy. He reached out and laid a hand on his shoulder.

"Tyler!"

Kent's concern was unfounded; as soon as his hand touched Tyler's Metallica T-shirt, the boy's eyes flipped forward again. Only this time the dark pupils were clear and lucid.

Tyler immediately shoved Kent's hand and arm away.

"What the fuck, Kent? What are you doing?"

Kent gaped.

What just happened? Was he dreaming? In a trance?

"I—I—" Kent stuttered, unable to get the words out.

Tyler rose from the log, his eyes narrowing.

"Did I say something?"

"I—"

"Did I say something about my dad, Kent?"

Kent shook his head slowly.

Tyler stared at him suspiciously.

"You sure? 'cuz whatever I said — "

Kent cleared his throat.

"You didn't say anything about your dad."

The boy still didn't appear convinced, but the confusion about what he was doing outside in the cold took hold and he decided to let it go.

"Then what the fuck are you doing here? Go to bed," Tyler ordered before turning and heading back to his own tent.

Kent stood there for a moment, alone in the moonlight, his hands hanging loosely at his sides.

Eventually the sounds of the forest returned.

What the fuck just happened? Who wants us to come?

8.

"THAT'S IT—YOU GUYS should be good to go," the mechanic informed them, pulling his head out of the boat engine.

Reggie stepped forward and took a rudimentary look at the man's work.

"Looks good," he announced to the group with an approving nod.

"Yep, should be good now for another couple hundred miles," the mechanic said, wiping his hands on a red rag. When he was done, he pushed the rag into the pocket of his soiled jeans. He was a round man with extra skin that folded about his chin and neck like a loosely tied bandana.

"Awesome, thank you." Gregory extended his hand. "What's your name, anyway?"

"Johnny," the man with the loose skin replied. "Johnny the Mechanic."

"Well, Johnny the Mechanic, thanks for the tune-up."

Despite the promise that the boat would be ready first thing in the morning, it was already half past nine. And if the sun that beat down on them at this early hour was any indication, it was going to be another scalding day.

"About time," Tyler grumbled, pulling himself onto the boat just as Johnny the Mechanic jumped off.

"Let's get this show on the road," Sergio added.

"Where are the life jackets?" Reggie asked.

Johnny stopped halfway down the dock and turned back.

"Should be in the cabin. Also, don't push the boat too hard, now. The engine will need a complete overhaul at the end of the season."

"Aye, aye, captain," Tyler whispered under his breath.

And with that, the mechanic left, making his way up the small embankment to his red pickup truck parked at the side of the road.

Kent and Sergio hopped onto the boat next, leaving only Nick and Baird on the dock. Gregory immediately went to the cabin and began his search for the life jackets.

"I'm going to catch me some dinner," Reggie said, rubbing his hands together. Then he turned his attention to the tacklebox on the seat beside him.

"Get on the boat," Tyler instructed Baird, enjoying

how the boy's face suddenly got serious.

Although the comment wasn't directed at him, Nick Salvado obliged, lowering himself onto the boat. It was a sleek twelve-foot pleasure craft, with a sleeping cabin that could accommodate three, if they were willing to share. Now, with all but Baird on board, Kent could see that they would have to share some *seats* as well.

Thoughts of last night in the tent with the boy flitted through his mind.

Please don't let me get stuck with Baird again.

He moved to the other side of the boat and took a seat as far away from the dock as he could.

"Baird?" Nick asked, turning to face the chubby boy.

When Baird looked hesitantly at the dock, then the boat, and then back at the dock again, Nick extended his hand.

"Come aboard, matey."

"This," Reggie interrupted, holding up a four-inch-long bright green-and-pink-spotted lure, "is gonna catch us enough dinner for the entire weekend."

Nick turned away from Baird and looked at him.

"Ha! And what are you gonna catch with that monstrosity? A whale?"

He chuckled as Reggie held the lure up to the sun, admiring the way the light reflected off the speckled surface.

"Nope. A Muskie; a giant muskellunge."

Nick shook his head and turned back to Baird, who had only taken one hesitant step toward the boat.

"Come aboard, Baird," he repeated.

Like a child testing the temperature of bathwater, Baird reached forward with his toe and then extended his hand. Just as their fingers met, Gregory came out of the cabin and Baird immediately pulled his hand back.

"Bad news, fellas," he informed them, holding a stack of yellow life preservers in his arms. "Can only find five life jackets."

Kent groaned.

"You sure?" Reggie asked, putting the massive lure back in the tacklebox.

Gregory nodded, his face grim.

"Looked everywhere."

"Lemme check," Reggie said, and Gregory turned to allow him to pass and enter the cabin.

Gregory tossed the life jackets on Reggie's abandoned seat and then flopped his body on the adjacent chair, clearly dejected.

"So?" Tyler asked, leaning forward. "Who cares?"

"I'll stay," Baird said quickly, and his face, unlike everyone else's, seemed to actually lift.

Gregory ignored both of their comments.

"I told them seven—*seven*—life jackets. Goddamn it."

"It's practically a yacht," Tyler offered. "Do we really need life jackets?"

Kent turned to his dad.

"Yeah, Dad, what gives? We can all swim."

He instinctively looked at Baird, and the boy quickly averted his eyes.

Or atleast float.

When Kent turned back to his father, he was surprised to see that the man was glaring at him, eyebrows furrowed.

Structure... rules to keep him straight.

Kent couldn't help but roll his eyes as he remembered his father's akward speech of a night ago. Gregory, on the other hand, was deadly serious. So serious, in fact, that he held Kent's gaze even as he replied to Tyler's original comment.

"Yes, Tyler, we all need life jackets."

Tyler frowned and slumped back into his seat. Although he only mouthed the words, Kent read them loud and clear: *Fucking life jackets.*

Reggie suddenly appeared from behind Gregory.

"No more," he said with a shrug. Unlike Kent's father, however, his tone wasn't so much languid as confused.

Reggie looked like he was going to add something else, but he caught the stern look on Gregory's face and decided against it.

For a few seconds, they all just stood or sat there, none of them sure of what to say.

Finally, it was Baird of all people who broke the silence.

"I'll stay," he repeated, then added, "besides, it's too late for fishing. They are cold-blooded, so—"

"Baird," his father said, and the boy's mouth snapped closed.

Gregory turned his gaze to the floor of the boat.

"Boys, I know this wasn't what we planned, but looks like you guys are gonna be stuck fishing from the dock today."

Kent immediately spoke up—he couldn't help himself.

"But Dad—"

Gregory shook his head.

"No, Kent, you guys have to stay here."

A tense silence ensued.

Fucking rules.

"Fine, I'll stay," Kent sulked.

Reggie's face changed as a thought came to him.

"Listen, boys," he began, a smile spreading on his face. He reached into his back pocket and pulled out his wallet. "Whichever one of you catches the largest fish from the dock gets this Benjamin."

He pulled a one-hundred-dollar bill from his wallet and held it up to the sun.

Without hesitation, Tyler reached over and snatched it from his hand.

"I'm staying," he said with a smile.

*   *   *

None of the boys caught anything larger than a small sunfish, but it didn't matter; the one-hundred-dollar bill was stuffed firmly into one of Tyler's pockets, and Kent knew that there was no way any of them would ever see it again—regardless of what size fish they caught.

Maybe because of this, or more likely because of the heat from another day that was melting into the mid-nineties, they had all given up fishing after only about an hour. The four of them—Sergio, Kent, Baird, and Tyler—sat on the dock, all of them shirtless except for Baird. Even Tyler had removed his beloved Metallica T-shirt, his ribs poking out from beneath his thin skin like bicycle spokes.

"Hey," Tyler suddenly said, turning to face Baird, who was sitting on the dock only a couple paces from the shore, "how does it feel to be named Beard, and yet all you can grow is that shit smear on your upper lip?"

Kent couldn't help himself—he laughed. The comment had been so sudden, so *unprovoked*, that it even brought a smile to Sergio's usually flat expression.

Baird looked at the three of them, his face contorting into a pout.

And I look like baby when I pout? Kent thought, observing Baird. The boy's round face was like a red tennis ball—minus the furry covering, as Tyler had so acutely pointed out.

Then Baird surprised everyone by responding.

"Okay, first of all," he said in his high-pitched voice, "my name is not Beard—its Baird. And who are you? Rip van Winkle? What kind of beard can you grow?"

Tyler laughed and went back to staring out at the calm water that lapped at the dock. In the distance, Kent picked up some whitecaps that would soon make their way to shore. Despite the stillness of the air, or perhaps because of it, he thought there might be a storm on the horizon.

"Who the fuck is Rip van Dinkle?" Tyler asked, not bothering to turn back to Baird. "That a boyfriend of yours?"

"...van Winkle," Baird corrected him.

"Who gives a shit? Nice mustache."

Tyler pulled a cigarette out of the pack and struggled to light it in the wind.

Kent looked at Baird. The boy actually looked like he was thinking about a witty retort, some dig to get back at Tyler. Baird's beady eyes bounced quickly from Kent to Sergio to Tyler.

Bad idea, Kent thought. *Keep your mouth shut, Baird.*

"Stop bitching, guys," Sergio said, spitting over the edge of the dock.

It was hot, and they were all irritable—the whole point of the trip had been to go fishing with their fathers. Instead, they were stuck on the dock with each other, bored out of their minds.

"Fuck you, Sergio—fuck you and your Tilley hat."

Sergio, who had at least ten inches and twice as many pounds on the much smaller Tyler, swore and went to stand, but Kent and grabbed his friend's arm before he made it to his feet.

"Fuck off, all of you," Kent said, trying to defuse the situation. "You all sound like bitches."

Tyler turned to him. His eyes were dark, and his furrowed brow caused the scar on the right side of his face to crinkle. When he frowned, as he was doing now, he looked much older than his sixteen years.

"And you have no soul, Ginger," Tyler said, but his eyes had softened and Kent let it go—he had been called worse.

Now that the attention was off him, Sergio also relaxed and went back to sitting on the dock, his hands stretched out behind his back.

The four of them sat there for a few minutes in silence, staring out over the water.

"I'm bored," Tyler said finally.

Sergio spat over the dock again.

"I'm borrrred," Tyler repeated. He turned to face Kent. "Let's play *Ba di ba*."

Sergio and Kent exchanged looks.

"What's *Ba di ba*?" Baird asked, but his query went ignored.

Sergio smiled.

"Well, you suggested it, so you get to go first," he said, directing the comment at Tyler. His voice was laced with venom, clearly still annoyed by the boy's previous insult.

Tyler shrugged.

"Fine—I always win anyway."

"Guys, what's *Ba di ba*?" Baird asked again.

"Okay," Sergio said with a smirk. "I have the perfect spot."

Kent followed his gaze out over the water to where the whitecaps started to break—they were getting closer to shore with every passing minute.

"Bring it," Tyler challenged, pulling another cigarette from the pack at his side.

*   *   *

"You ready?"

Kent could hear Tyler take three big gulps of air.

"Yeah, I'm ready," he replied. "Let's get this shit started."

Kent and Sergio were still sitting on the edge of the dock, while Baird had moved from the shore to join the other boys and was lying on his stomach, peering down between the wooden boards. Even sitting with his legs hanging over the edge, his bare feet tickling the water, Kent could make out the tip of Tyler's nose and his dark hazel eyes looking straight up at them from beneath the dock.

"Fucking spiders everywhere," Tyler grumbled. "C'mon, Gingie, get this fucking thing started."

Kent looked over at Baird as if to say, *Pay attention, your turn will come.* Then he peered down at Tyler between the wooden slats.

"*Ba di ba,*" he said slowly.

Even through the boards, Kent could see Tyler roll his eyes.

"*Ba di bo,*" he replied.

"*Ba di ba,*" Kent said again.

"This is a fucking piece of cake. I can't believe that this is the best you could come up with."

Sergio shook his head.

"*Ba di ba,*" Kent repeated more slowly this time.

"*Ba di bo,*" Tyler replied.

Baird had a confused look plastered on his round face.

"This is it? This is the game?"

Kent nodded.

"*Ba di ba.*"

"*Ba di bo.*"

"Well when does it end?"

He looked less than impressed.

"You'll see," Sergio replied.

"That's three," Tyler said from beneath them. His face was becoming strained—clearly, holding his body pressed to the underside of the dock was wearing on him. And he still had twenty-two to go.

"You can't—" Sergio began, but Tyler interrupted.

"C'mon, let's keep this rolling."

"*Ba di ba.*"

"*Ba di bo.*"

*   *   *

More than a half hour had passed with Tyler beneath the dock. The tips of his fingers that pushed up through the slats had become purple and wrinkled. With the boy's face still pressed up against the underside of the dock, Kent could see that his expression was twisted into a sneer. The tide had risen more than two feet, and storm clouds had slowly rolled in, bringing with them choppy waves. Every so often, the waves completely covered Tyler's face, before being washed away again.

"*Ba di ba,*" Kent said.

"*Ba di bo,*" Tyler replied immediately, his teeth starting to chatter.

Sergio smiled—he was enjoying this. In fact, Kent was getting his kicks, too.

"Getting cold under there, Tyler?"

Tyler said nothing.

"*Ba di ba.*"

"*Ba di bo.*"

"Guys, the tide is rising," Baird informed them.

The boy's arms were crossed over his chest, and Kent could see goosebumps on his pale forearms. It was just past noon, and had to be at least a hundred degrees out, and yet Baird was shivering—he was scared. Only Kent didn't know if he was scared for what was happening to Tyler or frightened of the possibility that he too might have to endure a round of *Ba di ba.*

"It's almost over," Kent said, deliberately drawing out the words.

Baird glanced down at Tyler's face pressed up against the underside of the dock, then back at Kent's grin.

"*Ba di—*" Baird started, but Sergio cut in, shaking his head.

"Nope—you can't do it. Kent started it, so only he can finish it."

Kent's smile grew and he turned back to Tyler.

"How many is it now?" Kent asked.

Eat my perfect marshmallow, will you?

"Oh, I dunno," Sergio replied slowly, looking skyward. He brought a finger to his chin and tapped it dramatically. "Twenty-one? No, that can't be it," he shook his head. "Twenty-three?"

"It has been exactly twenty-four '*Ba di bos*'," Baird replied quickly.

Sergio made a face.

"*Ba di ba?*" Kent asked at long last.

"*Ba di* fucking *bo*," Tyler replied.

Kent gave him a pass on that one.

"All right, Tyler, you win." Then to the others he said, "C'mon, guys, let's help get this Popsicle out of the water."

9.

THE BOAT RETURNED APPROXIMATELY two hours after the boys had finished their lunch, and they were all back on the dock waiting for it. As it neared, they could see the outline of a figure standing at the back of the boat, a shadow in the bright sun. When the boat coasted nearer, they realized that the shape was Reggie's muscular body.

"Wahoo!" the man shouted as he scampered toward the front of the boat. "I got the big one, boys!"

Reggie's face was plastered with a smile so large that Kent thought that if it grew anymore, his face might split in two. Now within a couple dozen feet from the dock, he raised his right hand. Judging by the strain on his still smiling face, the gesture took considerable effort. The man's fingers were buried deep in the gills of a massive gray fish—a Muskie that was at least four feet long. The fish was so heavy that the muscles on his bare chest and his arms flexed, the veins popping from his glistening flesh.

Tyler, having long since recovered from being submerged beneath the dock, stared in awe.

"Holy shit!"

"Yeah, baby!" Reggie beamed. He tried to hoist the massive fish up over his head, but even for him, his large bicep bulging, it was too heavy to lift one-handed. He settled for showing it off at eye level.

"Dad!" Baird exclaimed. "That's amazing!"

"Wow," Sergio and Kent said in unison.

It was the largest fish any of them had ever seen.

As Gregory pulled the boat up to the dock, Reggie lowered the fish back into the cooler, a satisfied grunt escaping him as his muscles got a reprieve from the heavy fish. It was so large that only the fish's thick middle fit inside the cooler, with the head and tail hanging limply out of either end. When Reggie raised his hand again, he held another fish between thumb and forefinger—a small green fish with pink flecks.

"And I caught it with this!" he shouted, holding the lure up to the sun.

Kent squinted and looked away as the lure caught the sunlight and reflected directly into his eyes.

"What did you say I was going to catch with this?" Reggie hollered over his shoulder to Nick Salvados.

"A whale," the man replied, the words coming out in

a puff of smoke. Nick pulled the cigar from the corner of his mouth. "I said you were gonna catch a whale."

Reggie laughed.

"I think what you said was, 'What do you *think* you are gonna catch with that? A whale?'" He chuckled again. "Naw—just a fifty-pound Muskie, baby!"

Nick, smiling now, jammed the cigar back into his mouth and went back to dealing with another cooler, the contents of which were out of sight to the boys on the dock.

"Grab the bow, Kent!" Gregory hollered from the stern.

Kent, still in shock at the sight of the massive fish hanging out of the cooler, quickly made his way to the front of the boat. Reaching over the water, he grabbed the rope that hung from the deck and pulled, easing the pleasure craft to the dock. When the white buoy on the side squeezed against the dock, he tied it up. A moment later, the back end coasted up to the dock and Sergio tied that end up as well.

Even before the boat came to a complete stop, Reggie disembarked, indicating for Sergio and Tyler to grab the cooler that he had pushed to the edge of the deck.

"Hot one out there today, eh, boys?" he said, slapping Sergio's bare back as he hopped passed them.

"Shit yeah," Tyler replied, his eyes transfixed on the muskellunge.

Sergio and Tyler leaned over the boat, each grabbing one side of the cooler. With a grunt, they lifted it up over the bow and dropped it heavily onto the dock. Nick Salvados, cigar still jammed in the corner of his mouth, jumped off next, landing heavily with two feet, and Baird, hanging close to shore, grabbed the handrail, his eyes bulging in fear.

"Check it out, boys!"

Reggie nudged Sergio and Tyler to one side, then reached into the cooler to once again pull out and display his prize. It was even more impressive close up, and the boys' jaws dropped.

"Awesome," Tyler uttered, leaning over Sergio's shoulder to get a better look.

Including the dark yellow tailfin, the fish was close to four and a half feet long, thick through the entire body, tapering only as it reached the final few inches before the tailfin and the dramatic underbite of its mouth. The length of its body was a pale green and brown and was covered in what looked like brown camo flecks, forming incomplete stripes that stretched vertically around its girth. With its tapered head and a row of large, irregularly placed teeth, it looked like a prehistoric beast.

"Yep," Reggie said proudly, relishing their awestruck expressions. "Pretty effing awesome, if you ask me."

Kent blinked hard. It was not only the largest fish he had ever seen, it was the *scariest* fish he had ever seen.

"Can I hold it?" Tyler asked almost breathlessly.

"You can try," Reggie replied, groaning dramatically as he handed it over the skinny boy.

The tail fell to the dock with a dull *thwack*, and Reggie

had to keep his hand around its middle to keep the fish upright. Tyler repeatedly tried to grab it by the gills with one hand, as Reggie had done, but failed; it was just too heavy for him. In the end, with Reggie's help, he resigned to holding it pressed against his chest, both arms wrapped around its middle.

"Jesus! It must be at least a hundred pounds!"

Reggie, who was standing behind the boy as if he might topple any second, laughed.

"Maybe not a hundred…"

The sound of the engine behind them suddenly cut out, drawing their attention away from the fish.

"Hey, guys," Gregory said, making his way to the front of the boat, "I know these aren't Jaws, but give me a hand with the other cooler full of fish, would you?"

*   *   *

" —at least two hours," Reggie said as he drove the paring knife into the fish just behind the gills.

Gregory rolled his eyes.

"No, I swear, I struggled with this beautiful beast for about two hours. The bastard went deep into the weeds by the shore—only about a foot of water—and I thought for a while that I had lost him."

He flipped the fish over and made a parallel cut on the other side.

"But then, thanks to my skipper Gregory over there, we moved the boat, and I managed—little by little—to ease him out into deeper waters. It was just a matter of time; no matter how much my arms burned, I was not going to lose him—this was a catch of a lifetime, I could just feel it."

With a flick of the knife, the fish's head was removed from its body. The fish's gaping mouth looked even more frightening now, the ragged area behind the gills trailing a pink-and-white mess of fat and muscle and a streak of blood.

Sergio, Tyler, and Kent watched as Reggie made quick work of the rest of the fish, first gutting it, then carving two massive filets. When he was done, he raised his face to the spectators, sweat glistening off of his handsome features in the fading sunlight.

"We are gonna eat like kings tonight, boys."

And eat they did.

*   *   *

After gorging themselves on barbecued Muskie and baked potatoes, the seven of them sat around the campfire, only this time there were no marshmallows. Even Baird, he of the bottomless stomach, he who was destined to be diabetic, opted against having something sugary after devouring at least a pound of the delicious fish.

"Damn," Reggie said with a tone that could only be described as languid, "what a day."

"Hear, hear," Nick replied, leaning back and lighting

up another cigar.

"Moby Dick caught his whale," Reggie sighed.

It was a warm night, the storm that had been brewing at noon having graciously passed them by. But despite the temperature, the mosquitos were so fierce that they all suffered in sweatshirts and jeans—even Tyler had changed out of his beloved Metallica shirt.

"Moby Dick was the *whale*," Baird corrected his father.

Reggie shook his head.

"Not this time."

Baird, his lips shining with grease by the light of the campfire, opened his mouth to say something, but then decided against it.

"Well," Gregory said, changing the subject, "who's up for some music?"

Although they all agreed, their enthusiasm was tempered by the vast quantity of fish they had consumed.

It was Metallica all night long.

10.

TYLER WAS THE ONE that suggested they kick off early.

"I'm bushed," he said, staring intently at Kent. "I think I'm gonna turn in for the night, boys."

Gregory stared at him for a moment, a confused look on his face, before he finally nodded and put his guitar away.

"Not a bad idea," he agreed, his eyes still trained on Tyler. "I managed to talk the manager at the campsite into picking up another few life jackets for tomorrow so you guys can join us on the boat."

"Great," Kent exclaimed, turning to Baird. As expected, the boy's round face, flickering with the light from the glowing fire, turned sour.

Buck up, Baird.

"Well," Reggie said, leaning backward on his log. He groaned as he interlaced his fingers behind his head. "I don't know if I'll go."

Nick groaned.

"We're never going to live this one down, are we?"

"What?" Reggie replied, sitting back up and feigning ignorance, the palm of one hand coming to his chest. "I mean, I caught my Moby Dick; what else do I have to accomplish? I should just retire."

Gregory snapped his guitar case closed.

"Oh, you're coming all right. And I'll bet you another one of those crisp hundreds that tomorrow I catch the biggest fish."

Reggie guffawed.

"Good luck."

"But," Gregory said with great emphasis, "this time you have to drive the boat."

Reggie submitted by holding up his hands.

"Sure" —he licked his lips— "but no way you catch something as big as the fish I caught today, because—"

Gregory opened his mouth to say something, but Reggie continued before he had a chance to interject.

"—because," he continued, "they just don't exist."

"Well," Gregory replied, rolling his eyes, "on that note, I am off to bed."

*   *   *

It was less than an hour after they had put out the

campfire that Kent heard a scratching sound at the door of his tent.

Kent leaned over and unzipped it and was greeted by Tyler and Sergio's smiling faces.

"They're all asleep," Tyler said, leaning into the tent with the bottle of vodka as he had the night before.

"How can you tell?" Kent said, rubbing his eyes.

"Snoring like motherfuckers," Tyler replied with a sly grin.

Kent looked over at Baird beside him, whose eyes were still closed, his mouth propped open slightly from the retainer.

"So is Baird."

Tyler shrugged.

"Leave him."

Sergio leaned into the tent and grabbed Baird's ankle through the sleeping bag. A bubble of snot that had formed outside his right nostril was quickly inhaled and he coughed. His eyes sprang open.

"Baird, wake up, man."

"What? What's going on?"

"Fuck," Tyler grumbled.

"Get up," Sergio continued, ignoring Tyler.

"Why? Where we going?"

Tyler popped the top to the vodka and took a swig. Unlike yesterday, this time he managed to suppress a grimace.

"To have a drink," he said, wiping his lips with the back of his hand. "Now get your pajamad ass out of bed and let's go."

Baird look dubious, confused, and a little scared, but he surprised them all by pulling down his sleeping bag and getting ready to rise without further hesitation.

Kent flipped back his own sleeping bag, but unlike Baird he was still in his clothes.

"Let's do this," Kent said, grinning.

The boys went down to the dock first. Even Baird sat near the end this time, legs dangling over the edge — maybe he was trying to look tough, or maybe it was his sleepy state that made him brave. Nevertheless, his attempts at looking tough failed horribly: he looked even more ridiculous than usual in his blue cotton pajamas that could have been worn by a seven-year-old — a massive seven-year-old with a round belly that stretched the fabric near the zipper. It was such a childish outfit that Kent wouldn't have been surprised if the boy's pajamas ended in booties, but with his thick hiking boots laced to the top, it was impossible to tell. He had to give the kid credit, though, as when the vodka as passed to him, he at least let the liquid hit his lips before passing it on. Sure, he stopped just short of swallowing, but Kent had to give him *some* credit for trying.

Tyler lit a cigarette and toed the water with a worn high-top.

"Where'd you get this shit from, anyway?" Sergio asked, bringing the bottle to his lips.

It was Kent who answered.

"Tyler took it from his mom when she was passed

out—all drugged up," he said, his tongue loosened by the alcohol.

His grin faltered when Tyler turned to face him. Despite his lack of size—even a bulky sweatshirt did nothing to hide his thin frame—the scar on his face made him look sinister. And now, sneering at Kent, his expression was clear—*don't fuck with me*—and he was an intimidating sight. Tyler never spoke much of his family, and when he mentioned his mother, it was usually something sarcastic or obtuse. And his father? Tyler had never mentioned him. But when he had taken his shirt off earlier in the day, they had all taken note of the criss-crossed scars across his back—long, smooth stripes that ran from beneath one arm to the other—and these said more than any words. These scars, like the one that ran down his face, were never spoken of, either.

"Don't make fun of my mom," Tyler warned.

Kent leaned away, defensive.

"You said it, man."

"Don't make fun of my mom," he repeated, his voice laced with vitriol.

Kent was about to say something, but thought better of it and closed his mouth.

Tyler, eyes still locked on Kent's, grabbed the bottle from Sergio and took a long swig before handing it back.

"Sorry," Kent grumbled, and averted his eyes.

The bottle did a couple more rounds as they stared at the reflection of the stars in the lake in silence. When Tyler spoke again, any trace of intimidation had long fled his voice.

"Let's play."

"Play what?" Baird asked. It had been a while since the boy had spoken, and Kent was beginning to think based on the way his words ran together that perhaps the vodka had touched more than his lips.

Sergio grinned.

"Why, *Ba di ba*, of course," Tyler said with a laugh, "and I think I know whose turn it is."

*　　*　　*

They had been walking for almost an hour, which had become a game in and of itself: every time Baird complained, they walked a bit further, a bit faster. And despite Baird's aversion to the vodka, he seemed to have a penchant for whine.

"Guys, I'm tired and covered in burrs."

Kent looked back at the chubby boy and laughed out loud—he couldn't help it. Baird's pale blue cotton pajamas were absolutely covered in burrs. He looked like a Hollywood movie star acting in front of a green screen covered in reflective balls. Except that he was chubby, uncoordinated, and a coward, and not a burgeoning action star.

"Almost ther—"

But Sergio stopped short as they pulled into a clearing, making it seem like they had reached a preordained location, when the truth was they had just been wandering aimlessly through the woods.

Tyler grabbed the bottle from Sergio and took another sip. It was almost empty now.

"There," he finished for Sergio, pointing with a finger that unfurled from the vodka bottle.

Sergio spun the flashlight across the lawn, illuminating several sticks that peppered the expansive clearing like odd, branchless saplings. Beyond the lawn was a massive house bathed in moonlight, the front door boarded up with a sheet of rotting plywood. The awning and door frame were charred from a fire that must have happened years ago.

Despite Tyler's enthusiasm, Kent didn't like the look of the place.

Come

"Yeah, I don't—" Kent began, but Tyler had already bounded up ahead and was nearly out of earshot. Kent looked to Sergio for support, but the boy simply shrugged and hurried after Tyler.

At the stairs leading up the porch, Tyler turned and looked back at them. He had that ominous look on his face again, and with the moonlight reflecting off his scar, it looked like it was glowing.

"C'mon, you pussies, you coming?"

None of the other boys moved—even Sergio had stopped halfway between Kent and the Estate.

"Fine," Tyler said, "I'll go in alone."

As if to prove his point, he turned and quickly made

his way up the porch.

Sergio and Kent exchanged looks—despite his previous indifference, it was clear that Sergio had changed his mind about the place. It wasn't just that the place was boarded up, that they were all a little drunk, and that the house had previously been involved in some sort of fire—it was something else. There was something wrong about this place—a sensation that lingered like a bad smell.

"There was a fire," Baird whispered from behind them and Sergio whipped the flashlight around.

No shit.

The boy's eyes were wide, his mouth slack.

"It could be dangerous," he added.

Sergio turned the flashlight to Tyler, who had made his way to the plywood-covered door.

Kent remembered what his dad had said the other night, and frowned.

Offer him a place where he can fit in, feel welcome.

He shook his head.

Fuck.

Knowing that he wasn't going to convince Tyler to leave the place, Kent took two hesitant steps toward the house.

"Yo, Tyler, wait up!" he heard himself say as he broke into a jog, pulling a reluctant Sergio with him.

After a dozen or so steps, Sergio stopped and turned the flashlight back toward Baird.

The boy still looked terrified, but his eyes were downcast as if he were contemplating his options. When he eventually took a couple of tentative steps toward them, Kent surmised that he had decided that staying on the lawn in the dark covered in burrs was a worse option than entering the abandoned house with his friends.

When all four of them finally made their way up the porch, Tyler turned and sized up the piece of plywood.

"We can pull it off," he said to himself, nodding.

"But do we want to?" Sergio asked.

"No, we definitely don't want to," Baird said from behind them, but like the vast majority of his inane commentary, this went ignored as well.

Kent turned his attention back to the doorway. The nails that held the wood in place were rusted, and at least half of them had worked their way almost completely out of the rotted plywood.

"There is police tape here, too," Kent noted.

"What, this?" Tyler replied, picking up a piece of torn tape that hung on either side of the doorway. "Look, it's all faded and grungy... probably been here for a hundred years."

Indeed, the yellow police tape had turned a pale green, and the words 'Do Not Enter' were faded almost to the point of being illegible.

"Help me get the wood off," Tyler said, turning his attention back to the door frame. Sergio shone the flashlight on Tyler's fingers and eventually they found purchase.

In the end, Tyler didn't need any help; the wood was even more rotted than it looked, and the remaining nails that held the plywood in place came out with ease. So easily, in fact, that Tyler had to lunge backward to avoid being hit by the massive piece of plywood as it crashed unexpectedly to the porch.

The loud bang that ensued skipped across the lake and echoed off the trees, and they all froze.

And waited.

After about a minute, Tyler's shocked expression became a grin.

"See?" he said to the group, "Ain't nobody around to hear us."

Baird looked skyward, his lips moving in silent prayer.

Tyler stepped to one side and waved a thin arm across the threshold.

"After you, ladies."

11.

IT WAS NEARLY PITCH black inside the Estate, as the
windows that flanked the front of the house, like the
front door, had also been boarded up. The only light was
a sliver of moonlight that spilled in from the doorway.

"Jesus," Sergio whispered, "it looks like no one has
been in here for years."

He swung the flashlight across the room, illuminating
the space in eerie lanes of blue light. They were in what
appeared to be a foyer, complete with two staircases that
wound their way to a landing high above them. The fire
that had started in the doorway had evidently spread to
the foyer, culminating in a large, charred smear in the
center. The wooden floor was as black as coal, the wood
warped and twisted, a few of the individual planks looking as frail and tenuous as spider webs in a windstorm.

"I don't think we should be in here," Baird whispered.

No shit.

"What is this place?" Kent asked.

No one answered.

Tyler, still a few paces further inside than any of the other boys, suddenly spun around. He was smiling.

"This is awesome!" he shouted.

Sergio sprayed his face with light, and Tyler shielded his eyes.

"Fuck, Sergio," he grumbled, but the smile remained plastered on his face. "Guys, this could be our place — our secret hideout."

It was a childish thing to say — *Welcome to our club, boys only* — but Kent thought he knew what he meant. It was like going back in time, nothing seeming to have been touched in years. It was strange, it was scary, but it was also exhilarating.

What happened here?

He bent and ran a finger across the floor beneath his feet. It came back charcoal grey.

"Look at this place — it's a mansion!" Tyler continued.

To reinforce his point, Tyler grabbed Sergio's hand holding the flashlight and directed it up to the landing.

Indeed, the place was massive, and despite the oddly confined burnt areas and the smell — a brooding funk, like the only intruder had been a family of raccoons that had found their way in, but had perished trying to escape — it appeared to be in pretty good shape.

"Let's go upstairs," Tyler said quietly, and despite Kent's unease, he agreed. Shit, they were already inside—what could it hurt to explore a little more?

Baird, on the other hand, was more hesitant.

"I'm tired," he said, feigning a yawn.

Tyler rolled his eyes.

"Head back if you want, pussy, but I'm going up."

Then he bolted, taking the stairs two by two, and Sergio and Kent had to sprint to the landing just to keep up.

"Wait up," Baird begged, before he too joined the other boys.

Once they had all congregated at the top of the stairs, they turned back to the foyer below.

"Awesome," Tyler muttered.

Kent placed two hands on the railing and peered over the edge. Tyler was right, the place was cool—huge and abandoned and *fucking* cool.

"Hey, you guys wait here for a second," Tyler added.

Catching Sergio by surprise, he snatched the flashlight from his hand and then faded into the dark recesses of the upper level.

"Tyler!" Kent hollered. "Tyler!"

But he was gone, and the boys resigned themselves to just standing there in the dark, listening to Tyler's receding footsteps.

"Tyler, get back here!" Baird squealed.

The shout echoed of the walls but went unanswered. After the words died, the house was eerily silent again— so quiet that Kent could hear Baird grinding his teeth.

Where the fuck did you go, Tyler?

Then he heard another sound, a strange rustling noise coming from where Baird had been standing.

"What is that?" Kent asked, his voice small.

No answer.

"Sergio? Baird?"

A bright light suddenly blanketed Kent and he immediately shielded his face. When his eyes finally adjusted to the light, he realized that it was just Baird; the boy had pulled out his cell phone and was shining it like a flashlight directly into his face.

"Baird!"

Kent looked at the boy, now bathed in a wash of light that illuminated his burr-covered pajamas.

Where the fuck was he keeping that? His pajamas have pockets?

Baird turned the light back to the foyer below them, concentrating the weak beam on the burnt scar in the middle.

"What do you think happened here?"

"Dunno," Sergio began, "Maybe—"

"Boo!"

All three of the boys jumped. Kent fell backward into Sergio, who caught him and pushed him back to his feet before they both went down. Baird dropped his cell phone, and it clattered loudly to the hardwood, the light blinking out.

Tyler burst out laughing, swinging the flashlight in a wide arc across their faces.

"You should see your faces!"

Tyler's laughter grew more intense, and soon he was doubled over, unable to control himself.

Sergio, the first to regain control of his faculties, reached over and punched Tyler on the shoulder, which only made him laugh harder.

"You should—" he repeated between gasps for air, "—you should see your faces."

He trained the flashlight on Baird, his hand twitching with the laughter that continued to course through him. The boy, who had yet to move, looked as if he had seen a ghost.

This brought forth another bout of laughter.

"Did you drop some mud in your jammies, Baird?"

Kent swore.

"What the fuck is wrong with you, Tyler?"

Tyler, still laughing, held out the nearly empty bottle of vodka, and Sergio took it from him. The boy's hands were shaking, and it took him several tries to remove the cap. Eventually, he managed a trembling sip, and offered the bottle to Kent first. Kent shook his head.

"Pick up your phone, Baird," Tyler said, finally recovering from his near seizure. "I found the perfect place to play."

*   *   *

"No way," Baird said.

"Yes way," Tyler responded.

They were standing in front of a charred doorway, the dim flashlight trained on the interior of the room. It was a nearly empty space, save a leather chair near the door. The back of the room was heavily burnt, a large black smear running from the back third of the room and up the entire wall. The floor looked wonky in places, and Kent thought that he could make out the floor beams in places where the boards had completely burnt away. Even the ceiling was charred.

"No."

Kent looked at the boy. He looked ridiculous in his burr-covered pajamas, his round moon face the height of terror. For a moment, Kent felt bad for him. But then he remembered how Baird had taken part, albeit reluctantly, when Tyler was beneath the dock. And, besides, no one had forced him to come with them; he could've just kept his retainer jammed in his mouth and gone back to snoring all night long.

Kent leaned toward the boy.

"Baird, you gotta play, man."

Baird shook his head vigorously.

"Hey, you thought it was all fine and dandy when I was playing," Tyler said. "Fucking giggling when I was drowning under the dock."

Baird shook his head again.

"C'mon, Baird," Kent said, "it's a fucking game. Just go in there—we'll be on the other side of the door. You just have to answer *Ba di bo* twenty-five times, then you can come out."

"Or you can be a big fucking pussy and don't answer us three consecutive times," Tyler added, "but then you don't get to play again." He paused, his eyes twinkling by flashlight. "Ever. And—"

Kent raised his hand and Tyler surprised him by shutting up.

"Baird, you gonna do it or what?" he asked.

Kent could literally hear the boy's mind churning as he thought it over, his face blank. Another pang of guilt shot through him as he realized that the chubby, uncomfortable kid had probably been excluded from nearly every game growing up.

Last pick for kickball.

Baird twitched, and Kent leaned closer, indicating that Sergio should focus the light on him.

"Baird?"

Then he twitched again, and Kent realized that the tic had actually been a nod; a subtle, nearly imperceptible movement, but a nod nonetheless.

"Good. Consider this your... your, uh, your *initiation*," Sergio added.

The initiation of the uninitiated, Kent thought. *Peer pressure at its finest.*

Then, to make sure that the boy didn't change his mind, he rested his hand on the small of Baird's burr-covered back and gently encouraged him toward the open doorway.

"Just twenty-five times, okay?"

Baird's eyes were still wide, but this time he nodded

more perceptibly. With his hand clutching his phone—
which wouldn't turn on again after having been
dropped—so tightly that Kent thought he might crush
the plastic case, he turned and took one hesitant step toward the door. Then he stopped and reached out to Sergio, beckoning for the vodka. Sergio grinned and passed
him the bottle. Baird took a big swig, grimaced, gasped,
and then wiped the vodka that dribbled down his chin
before handing it back. His hand was shaking. The boy
nodded again, this time more to himself than to the others, and put a foot inside the doorway.

"What happened here?" he whispered absently, but
before anyone could answer, Tyler stepped forward and
shoved him into the room.

Baird cried out and fell to one knee just as Tyler
slammed the door closed behind him.

12.

"BA DI BA?" TYLER asked.

They were all sitting on the floor of the upper level of the charred Estate, Tyler with his back leaning against the blackened, closed door. The vodka continued to make its rounds, their once enthusiastic gulps having since eased into small sips in an attempt to keep the bottle from running dry.

"It fucking stinks in here," Baird whispered. It was obvious by the clarity of his voice that he was also pressed up against the door—the other side of the door—trying to keep as far away from the burnt smear at the back of the room as possible.

Tyler raised an eyebrow.

"Ba di ba?"

When there was no immediate answer, Tyler reached

back and slammed the heel of his hand against the door. The loud bang resonated throughout the empty house and they all jumped. Kent thought he heard Baird whimper.

"Jesus—"

"Just answer, Baird," Kent said.

"Ba di bo! Ba di fucking bo!"

Tyler smiled.

"What do you think happened?" Sergio asked. Although this was the third or fourth time that the question had been posed, this was the first time that it was asked by someone other than Baird, and thus it deserved an answer.

Kent shrugged.

"No idea. Actually, I'm not really sure where we are, to be honest with you."

Tyler spoke up.

"Askergan County," he replied bluntly. "And I think I know what happened here."

He grinned again, and smacked his heel against the door a second time.

"Ba di ba?"

"Ba di bo," Baird answered immediately.

It was going to be a long night.

*   *   *

Kent didn't believe any of Tyler's story—it was just too fantastical, a typical campfire ghost story. But when he racked his brain, he thought he remembered something about a small town sheriff being killed along with a bunch of Askergan residents. Some sort of serial killer who liked to skin his victims—or, at least, that's what his vodka-laced mind remembered. He had only been nine or ten at the time he had first heard the story, and even then he had chalked it up to the newest version of 'Bloody Mary', a warning not to head out into a blizzard. Nevertheless, sitting here in the dark, in a huge mansion with a collection of odd, burnt smudges, was enough to give him pause—and evidently Sergio too, as after Tyler completed his tale, the two of them sat in silence for nearly five minutes.

Baird, on the other hand, was nearly in tears, his constant whimpering leaking through gaps in the burnt door. Despite his whining, Kent had to give the boy credit—he had held out for much longer than he, or any of them, would have thought. Driven by the thought of being part of the group—of fitting in with them, with someone, no doubt.

Kent turned to Tyler, who was still grinning, the scar on his cheek splitting his face in half. It was a farce; Baird would never fit in with them, and especially not with Tyler. As he watched Tyler toy with the flashlight, trying to keep the light from fading, he started to think that maybe none of them really fitted in with Tyler.

He had a hard life, his dad had said, and only now did Kent fully realize what the man had meant.

The physical scars on his body weren't the only impressions that his upbringing had made on him.

"Hey... hey, guys?" Baird whispered from the other side of the door. "Do you guys hear that?"

Kent listened closely. All he could hear was the sound of Baird's wet breathing.

"No."

It was Sergio who answered, but despite the directness of his response, Kent thought he detected a waver in his voice.

"It sounds like—" Baird hesitated, his voice becoming taut. "Oh god—it sounds like someone cracking their knuckles."

"You're the one who is fucking cracking," Tyler replied, still grinning. Then he added, "*Ba di ba?*"

"Oh god," Baird whispered, "there it is again, that... cracking... Don't you hear it?"

Kent actually thought he had heard something this time, but to him it just sounded like the old, burnt floorboards creaking.

Someone cracking their knuckles?

"*Ba di ba?*" Tyler repeated a second time.

A part of Kent wished Baird would just wait for one more so that they could just get the hell out of this creepy house.

What the fuck are we doing here?

"Baird," Sergio whispered, taking another sip of vodka, "you better answer."

"*Ba di bo,*" Baird moaned.

The boy was crying again.

*   *   *

When Kent finally pulled the door open, after Tyler's final and cruelly drawn-out *Ba di ba*, Baird practically fell on top of him. The boy's eyes were wide, and his face — all of it, from his lips to his forehead — was wet and glistening in the light from the now nearly dead flashlight. He was absolutely terrified.

Tyler laughed.

"You did it," Kent said, awkwardly pushing the boy off of him. "You passed."

Tyler scoffed.

"Passed? You mean pissed... look at him — probably pissed himself."

Kent frowned, yet despite his disapproval of Tyler's comment — *Jesus, hasn't the boy been through enough?* — he couldn't help but look down at Baird's burr-covered pajamas. Even by the dying flashlight, he recognized a dark spot around his crotch — one that grew as he watched.

Shit.

He really had pissed himself.

Tyler noticed the stain around the same time and he took a step back, pointing.

"Look!" he shouted, his outstretched finger aimed at Baird's crotch. "Look! He *did* piss himself!"

Sergio's face contorted in disgust, and Baird bowed his head in shame.

"Gimme that bottle," Tyler demanded, and snatched the vodka from Sergio's hand. There was only a sip or two left.

He finished it.

Kent yawned and rubbed at his eyes; the day had been long and hot, and like the flashlight, he was starting to fade.

"Anybody have the time?" he asked.

The sky outside had become overcast, the moon and twinkling stars no longer visible through the open doorway below them.

When no one answered, he turned to Baird and told him to take out his phone. At first, the boy didn't answer, resigning himself to keeping his head low and continuing to whimper.

"Oh, for fuck's sake, Baird! Get it together," Tyler said.

Baird sniffed hard, trying to collect himself, and slowly reached into his pajamas. Kent was slightly perturbed that Baird—who had been sleeping soundly before they had roused him—had kept his cell phone in his pajamas when he slept. And again Kent was struck by the strangeness of pajamas with pockets—what kind of pajamas have pockets?

Eventually Baird's fingers—moving painfully slowly—grabbed the phone, and he pulled it out of his pocket. As his trembling hand held it out to him, there was a loud *whoosh* sound to Kent's left, and he turned just in time to see the now empty vodka bottle careening through the air above their heads.

"Tyler!" he shouted, but the grinning boy ignored him, intent on watching the bottle tumble through the air, end over end.

Kent wasn't sure if he had missed the phone being handed to him or if Baird had simply dropped it when the empty vodka bottle exploded in the foyer below. Either way, Baird jumped backward at the sound and promptly fell on his ass. The chubby boy moaned in pain, but quickly scrambled back to his feet when he realized that he had fallen back into the foul-smelling room.

"What the fuck, Tyler!" Kent shouted.

Tyler reached into his pocket and pulled out a cigarette. When he finally finished the ritual of lighting it and raised his eyes, all three boys were staring at him, anger pasted on their faces.

"What?" he asked with a shrug.

Then he exhaled a large cloud of blue smoke that billowed about his face.

"It was empty."

13.

"WELL I'M NOT GOING anywhere," Tyler said petulantly. "Not just yet, anyway."

Kent opened his mouth to reiterate his desire to leave this place, but Tyler continued before he had a chance to speak.

"What's your problem, anyway, Kent? You want to head back now because you know it's your turn?"

Kent made a face and shook his head.

"Oh yeah, that's it, isn't it, Kent? Scared now because it's your turn?"

There was a gleam in his eyes that Kent didn't care for.

"I'm not scared," he said bluntly, and it was the truth. Yet while he wasn't really afraid, he was disturbed—very disturbed. The story that Tyler had told them wasn't—couldn't be—true, but there was something wrong with this empty house; the place wasn't quite right. It was the multiple burn marks throughout the house, as if the fire had been deliberately started in several places at once, and it was the sound that he had heard when Baird was alone in the room.

Disturbed. Yeah, that was a good word for it. Not scared; *disturbed.*

"Well then, my friend, I think it's your turn."

Kent shook his head.

"It's late—I'll play tomorrow."

Tyler made a face.

"How do you know it's late? Dumbass there"—he indicated Baird with a flick of his head—"dropped his phone and it won't turn on. Besides, you promised me."

"Fuck, I'm tired, the flashlight is low on batteries, and this place stinks. Let's play tomorrow."

Now it was Tyler's turn to shake his head. He was about to say something, when Baird surprised them all by speaking up.

"I did it," the boy said meekly.

Kent turned to face him, incredulous. Baird's eyes were downcast, and he was digging one of the toes of his boots into a charred floorboard. Kent had managed to convince them to come downstairs, and they were nearly out the front door—the ragged opening that Tyler had made by pulling off the rotted plywood—before *this*; before Baird of all people trying to pressure *him*.

"Baird? What the fuck?"

"I'm just saying," he whispered.

He didn't dare look at Tyler, didn't dare look over at the boy's shit-eating grin.

"Well," Sergio said, speaking up for the first time in several minutes. The word was slurred, and Kent could tell by the way the boy swayed slightly even though he was standing still that he was buzzed. "He's right. Baird did it. And it *is* your turn."

Kent's eyes went from Baird, to Sergio, and then back to Tyler. The latter pressed the flashlight to his chin, illuminating his face in a shadowy glow.

"You scared, little Kent?"

"Fuck off."

In the end, it was Baird's comment that cemented it.

One more round.

Kent shook his head and pressed his lips together.

Fucking peer pressure.

*   *   *

"No fucking way."

"Yes fucking way."

It was like déjà vu—only this time it was Tyler trying to convince Kent and not Baird.

Kent was staring into what could only be described as a dungeon, the dim flashlight—now starting to flicker—illuminating a set of wooden stairs that looked so rickety that an inquisitive fly might cause the entire staircase to collapse.

"I did it."

Baird again.

"Shut the fuck up, Baird," Kent nearly shouted.

They had found the trapdoor toward the back of the house in the kitchen when Baird had nearly tripped on a small brass ring that was nearly flush with the hardwood. The kitchen, unlike the foyer or the room upstairs, looked relatively untouched by the fire, and aside from the ubiquitous layer of dust, it looked pristine. But once they had opened that door — the trapdoor hidden in the hardwood — a waft of horrific-smelling warm gas told a completely different story. A story that Kent had no interest in reading the prologue of, let alone the ending.

"Kent," Tyler said, changing tactics, "take a drag of this cigarette."

Kent reached out and snatched the cigarette from Tyler and put it to his lips. He inhaled deeply, and when the harsh smoke hit his throat and then his lungs, he sputtered and coughed. He turned his head and spat phlegm on the floor, then took another drag. His head started to swim.

"Good," Tyler said. "We'll make this one quick, I promise." When he went to reach for his cigarette, Kent took a third drag, then flicked it to the ground.

"Here, take the flashlight," Tyler said, pulling another cigarette out of the pack.

Kent banged the head of the flashlight twice against

the palm of his hand to get it to stop flickering. Then he again turned the weak beam of light to the dungeon. Although he could barely make out the bottom of the stairs, the ground below looked like it was covered in dirt instead of concrete or hardwood.

Why the fuck am I doing this?

Still shaking his head, Kent extended his leg, his foot tentatively searching for the top stair. When his foot found purchase, the wood creaked but held.

"Oh, and Kent?" Tyler said.

Kent turned, hoping that Tyler had changed his mind and would tell him to get out of the fucking dungeon so that they could leave this place and make their way back to their respective tents.

Fuck him and fuck this game.

"You have to go to the bottom."

Kent swung the flashlight around again.

Eight steps—nine if you included the one he was presently standing on.

"All the way?" he asked, his voice sounding more like Baird's high-pitched whine than his own. He cleared his throat and asked again, more forcefully this time.

"All the way."

The smile had returned to Tyler's face. A grin. A fucking shit-eating grin.

Kent decided to just get it over with. It was just a house, after all. An old, abandoned, burnt, undeniably creepy fucking house—but just a house, nonetheless.

*   *   *

By the time he reached the bottom stair, the flashlight was nearly dead. Twice, he had to stop partway down, terrified that the rotted wood would collapse under his weight. When he finally jumped from the bottom step to the ground—which was indeed dirt—the pathetic beam of light from the flashlight had become so weak that he could only make out just about as much as he had from the top of the staircase. The basement wasn't empty, that much he could tell, but truth be told, Kent, his breathing shallow, didn't really want to know what kind of shit was down here. Instead, he turned his attention back up the staircase and into the kitchen.

"Okay, let's get this—"

But Tyler's face suddenly filled the opening—he was smiling again, that goddamn hideous scar parting his face in two—and then he slammed the trapdoor closed.

Kent was alone. His heartrate immediately kicked into high gear.

"Okay, let's go!" he shouted.

The sound echoed off the walls and low ceiling and slapped his ears.

He heard Tyler laugh but then, true to his word, he quickly got into the game.

"*Ba di ba?*"

"*Ba di bo.*"

The flashlight flickered and went out. This time, Kent decided not try to bang it back on. Instead, he clicked it off, deciding to let it recharge just a little so that he could use it to get back up the stairs later.

"*Ba di ba?*"

"*Ba di bo.*"

Kent was blanketed in an oppressive darkness, like being submerged in oil. There was no light, not even a sliver of illumination splaying through the seams of the trapdoor above.

This is nuts.

"*Ba di ba?*"

"*Ba di bo,*" Kent replied quickly.

Twenty-three to go.

It was after the sixth *Ba di ba* that Kent first heard it: a faint crackling noise, like someone stepping on dry leaves. His heartrate quickened and he whipped his head in the direction it had come, but he was still drowning in the oppressive darkness and saw nothing.

"Do you guys hear that? Sounds like something cracking..."

A rat. It was a fucking rat.

"*Ba di ba?*"

"*Ba di* fucking *bo.*"

"*Ba di ba?*"

Then he heard it again, a muffled cracking sound — and Kent knew then that it was definitely *not* a rat. It sounded like someone cracking their knuckles underwater.

"Fucking weird cracking sound."

The boys above ignored him.

"*Ba di ba?*"

"*Ba di bo.*"

As his ears slowly began to adjust to the silence, he thought he heard something else as well—an underlying rushing noise, like slowly boiling water.

He swallowed hard.

"Fuck me! There are fucking rats or something down here."

Not rats; rats don't make that sound.

Kent's breathing was coming in shallow bursts and his eyes, ineffective as they were in the complete darkness, were spread so wide that the corners of his lids started to hurt.

He soon lost count of how many *Ba di bas* had passed. Not enough—definitely not twenty-five.

"*Ba di ba?*"

A loud crack suddenly erupted from his left, and Kent jumped back onto the first step of the staircase.

"*Ba di—*"

When he lowered his hand to where he thought the wooden railing was, trying to make sure that he kept tabs on where he was, it landed on something soft—something soft and hairy, and he screamed.

"Oh my God," he gasped, "there is something down here with me!"

His heart thudded so strongly in his chest that he found it difficult to stand still without rocking. A cold sweat broke out on his face.

When the door at the top of the stairs didn't open immediately, Kent stumbled forward in the darkness, desperately probing for the bottom stair with an outstretched foot. He heard another crack, and his withering resolve snapped.

"Tyler, open the fucking door!" he screeched.

Kent fumbled with the flashlight, eventually managing to switch it on. The light was dim and yellow, but—*thank Christ*—it actually worked. He swung it in a wide arc behind him, but he saw only dirt and—and something else, right next to where he had stumbled only moments ago.

"Kent, you know what happens if you come out before the game's over," he heard Tyler say in his best patronizing tone. Kent ignored him.

There, just beyond his scrambled footprints in the dirt, was a shape—an oval covered in what looked like a thick comforter.

What the fuck is that?

"Tyler! Open the fucking door now!"

Heart thumping in his chest, he turned his attention back to the stairs, and when his foot finally found purchase, he jumped up to the second step, ignoring the wood's protests. Something heavy had been on this staircase before him, something so massive that it had loosened the nails and warped the boards.

The trapdoor finally opened and Tyler looked in. This time, however, he wasn't smiling.

"Kent—"

"Get me the fuck out of here!"

Tyler made a face, but he leaned into the basement to grasp Kent's arm with the intention of helping him out. It was then, just an instant before their fingers touched, that the entire staircase collapsed.

14.

DUST.

There was so much dust, and it was everywhere.

It was in Kent's eyes, a gritty layer that coated his corneas, forcing him to blink rapidly and continuously. It was in his mouth, drying it out and making swallowing a painful experience. It was in his nose, making it difficult to breath. It covered his entire body.

He was lying on his back, a piece of the stairs — a step, maybe, or part of the bannister — pressing into his spine. He thought he was staring upward at the ceiling, but he couldn't be sure; it was too dark and dusty to tell.

He shut his mouth, his tongue scraping at the earthy texture of the dirt, and forced air through his ears, making them pop. Almost immediately, his hearing cleared and he heard the voices.

"Tyler! Kent! You guys okay?"

It was Sergio's voice, and he sounded desperate.

Kent blinked again, and the grittiness faded somewhat as his eyes began to water—his vision, however, remained dark. A pain just above his left hip shot through him and he gasped, but it faded quickly. As he probed the tender area, he realized that one of his fingers must have been cut, based on the way his palm felt tacky when he made a fist. But—he slowly rolled onto his side, and then pushed himself onto his haunches—he thought that he had managed to avoid serious injury.

He coughed, the action forcing more sandy grit against the back of his teeth and onto his tongue. He spat.

"Tyler? Tyler, you okay?"

There was a sputtering, gasping sound from his right, and he turned toward it. Then he heard the other noise—the one from before, the one that sounded like someone quietly cracking there knuckles. It was hidden beneath his and Tyler's raged breathing, but it was *there*—quiet, subdued, but *there*.

"Tyler? Kent?" someone hollered from above.

Sergio. It was Sergio again.

"Yeah," Kent hollered back, "I'm all right—I think."

He did another cursory patdown of his body as if to convince himself. Aside from the pain in his left side and his sticky palm, he found no other source of injury—but, then again, he had only been on the third step when the staircase had collapsed; Tyler had been at the top.

"And Tyler?"

"I don't—"

Another sputter followed by a cough interrupted him.

"I'm here—I mean, I'm all right."

Tyler coughed again.

"My ankle is a bit fucked up, but I think it's just sprained."

"Fuck." Sergio let out a sigh. "That was fucked up."

"I knew we shouldn't have come here."

It was Baird's whiney voice.

Tyler groaned.

"Shut the fuck up, Baird."

Kent nodded.

Seriously, shut the fuck up.

Kent looked away from the barely recognizable shadow of a head peaking in from the opening to the floor above and tried to locate Tyler in the darkness. He heard movement, and thought he saw a shadow flicker to his left—and then he heard that cracking noise again.

"Stop cracking your damn knuckles, Tyler," he grumbled, bringing himself to his feet. His back was sore, too, he realized, but he was still amazed that he didn't seem to be seriously injured.

"I'm not fucking cracking my knuckles," Tyler replied.

Kent froze. Tyler's voice had come from his right, the cracking sound his left. He scrambled to his right, groping blindly for Tyler.

"What the fuck is that, then?" he whispered hoarsely, still moving to his left.

"A rat, maybe?" Tyler said, his voice now just a few feet from him. Kent jumped at the sound.

Rat—it's not a rat... that cracking... a rat doesn't have knuckles to crack.

"We have to get out of here," Kent said.

"No shit." Tyler grunted again. "Help me stand."

Kent took another shuffling step to his right and his outstretched arm finally found Tyler's head at roughly waist level. He squatted and wrapped his arm around the slender boy and helped him to his feet. Tyler leaned heavily against him, presumably to avoid putting any weight on his injured ankle.

"You guys all right?" Sergio asked again from above. The man's usually nearly infallible demeanor was beginning to falter; there was a hitch in his voice.

"We'll live," Tyler replied, then added, "could use some more of that vodka, though."

Kent ignored him, and again his attention was drawn to the shadowy figure above.

"How are we gonna get out of here?"

The cracking sound came again, and Kent's head snapped to his right. Only this time it didn't so much sound like knuckles, but a rhythmic snapping. Tyler must have heard it too, because his body, which was still propped up against Kent, tightened. Maybe Sergio and Baird had heard it as well, as they seemed to go quiet, but he thought not—the sound was distinct, but it wasn't all that loud.

There.

The sound repeated, and this time Kent counted.

One.

Two.

Three.

Four.

Five.

Six.

The cracks came at what sounded like regular intervals.

"That's no rat," Kent whispered, and a tremor coursed through him.

Tyler suddenly lurched in the direction of where the staircase had once hung, the urgency in his shuffled steps evidence that he didn't think it was a rat anymore either.

Together they hobbled forward, careful not to stumble over what was left of the stairs. Three steps, and Tyler cried out and started to fall.

"What happened?" Baird yelled.

Kent rooted his left foot and pulled back, trying to keep both of them from tumbling. Thankfully, he outweighed Tyler by a good fifteen pounds and he managed to right them. When he went to bring his right arm back to his side, it struck against something hard, something that felt like a handle. In his hyper-agitated state, he cried out.

"What?" Tyler demanded, his sour alcohol breath hot on his ear.

Kent took a deep breath.

"I dunno, some sort of handle."

The cracking sound returned—*crack, crack, crack*—and this time it sounded like it was coming from only a half dozen feet in front of them.

"A handle?" Tyler asked quickly, clearly trying to ignore the rhythmic cracking sound.

"I dunno," Kent replied, "let's keep moving."

But when he went to take another cautious step forward, trying to make his way to directly below the trapdoor, Tyler resisted.

"What is it?" he asked again. "Is it a handle?"

Annoyed and frightened, Kent reached out—hesitantly at first, worried that he might put his hand on the furry object again—but when he felt the familiar feel of cold metal, he ran his hand along its length. It ended in a rubber grip.

"Yes, a fucking handle, now let's get out of here."

Still, Tyler resisted.

"Fucking crank it!" the boy nearly shouted.

Crank it? What the fuck is he talking about?

"Let's just fucking go, man—let's get the fuck out of here."

Baird spoke then from above in his high-pitched voice.

"A lot of old places have crank generators, in case…"

Kent squeezed his eyes tight, ignoring the rest of the boy's commentary. He was nearly in tears now, as he had come to realize that climbing out of this hellhole was not going to be an easy feat—even if Tyler hadn't hurt his ankle.

"Turn it," Tyler said again, almost excitedly, and nudged Kent to his right.

Kent started to silently cry.

What is he talking about? Fucking turn it, fucking turn it—let's just get the fuck out of here!

"Turn it!"

Kent grabbed the handle and pushed. It was stuck.

"Turn it!"

"I can't!" Kent shouted, nearly sobbing. "It's fucking stuck!"

He felt Tyler reach across him, but before he fell and took Kent down with him this time, Kent pushed him back and drove the palm of his hand into the rubber grip again. This time, it moved a few inches, and he felt a small blast of air hit his side from beneath the handle. Tyler, who was now somehow in front of Kent, must have felt it too.

"It's a fucking crank generator," he said almost giddily. "Turn it, Kent."

A fucking crank generator? What the hell is a crank generator?

But he didn't have to ask the question, because Baird answered without initiation.

"A crank generator is a hand-powered generator," Baird replied, returning to his annoying *I'm smarter than thou* tone, and repeating pretty much what he had said moments ago when Kent had shut him out. "They have them sometimes in old places, usually close to where the real generator is located. The idea being that if the power goes out—"

"Shut the fuck up, Baird!" Tyler shouted.

Generator. Generator means light.

Kent pushed the handle again, and this time it moved a quarter turn. He pushed again, and again, and soon whatever rust had laid claim to this archaic device seemed to break away, making every subsequent rotation a little easier, a little more fluid.

"Turn it, Kent!" he heard Baird holler down at them.

Sweat was forming on his brow now, and it was immediately soaked up by the layer of dirt and dust, turning it into an uncomfortable paste.

The next push resulted in a full rotation, and Kent had to shift his grip to pull it up the other side. A dim glow suddenly leaked toward them, the weak light trying desperately to penetrate the cloud of dust that still hung in the air. Shocked, Kent let go of the handle and the light immediately vanished. It had been so weak and transient that his eyes hadn't been able to adjust in time to make out anything in the basement.

"Don't stop!" Tyler demanded, shoving him again.

Kent grabbed the handle and cranked it around in a full circle, this time adjusting his wrist to keep the movement going into another circle. Slowly, the dim glow returned, but instead of stopping, this time he kept turning.

"Yes!" Tyler cried, and Kent heard Sergio and Baird make similar affirmative grunts from somewhere above.

Faster and faster he turned the crank, the light growing in intensity with every rotation. Squinting, Kent started to make out several shadowy shapes. He also heard the scurrying noise again, and this reminded him of the rhythmic cracking sound.

Maybe I don't want to see.

But that was silly and childish—*Baird-like*—and he forced himself to continue cranking the handle despite his apprehension. The generator served another purpose, he realized; the room was no longer silent, the dusty air filling with the crackle of electricity and the whirring of the fan—which meant he could no longer hear the muted cracking sound.

As the light continued to penetrate the basement, Kent began to discern familiar shapes: the handrail, lying on the dirt ground; the wooden steps, scattered about the floor like smashed mahjong tiles. Part of the frame lay wasted on the floor only a couple of inches from his foot; it was a wonder that it hadn't landed on the crank generator when it had collapsed.

"What do you see? Can you get out?" Sergio called from above.

The truth was, Kent couldn't see much, what with the dust motes suspended in the air and the fact that Tyler was standing almost directly in front of him. With the arm not feverishly turning the crank, Kent gently nudged Tyler, and the boy obliged and moved to his left.

A single bare bulb hung from a thick black cable at the very back of the basement, illuminating a wall of red bricks behind it. The bricks appeared to glisten in the light, humidity beading on them like sweat. Kent's gaze slowly traveled from the back wall toward where they stood, and again his breath caught in his throat. His hand froze and the basement quickly went dark again.

"Don't turn it off," Tyler shouted, his voice desperate. *"Don't turn it off!"*

15.

KENT STARED WIDE-EYED at what looked like a dozen or so fur blankets stretching from just a few feet from where the last step of the stairs had been, all the way to the back wall. The blankets were thick and *hairy*, and as his bulging eyes scanned their surface, he noted a myriad of colors: dark grey, brown, and even black.

At first, he thought that the comforters were simply piled several feet high, hiding more blankets beneath, but as his eyes continued to adjust to the dim light, he realized that they were covering something else; a number of round shapes jutted from beneath, as if the patchwork of blankets had been stacked on top of several pillows.

It looked like discarded bedding.

But it wasn't.

The objects were too perfectly shaped, too round—in a word, they looked *organic.*

"What the fuck are they?" Tyler whispered.

Kent offered a grunt as a reply as he continued to ream the crank, trying to spin it faster and faster to generate more light. But no matter how quickly the crank turned, the glow from the bare bulb remained the same: dull and yellow.

For a moment, they just stared. Then Sergio spoke in a voice that didn't sound his own.

"Eggs?"

Kent's hand slipped and the light faded again. Somewhere above them, he heard Baird cry out. Fumbling in the darkness, his hand found the handle and began to turn it again.

Eggs.

A shudder ran through him.

"There," Tyler whispered, and Kent followed his friend's outstretched finger.

When the stairs had collapsed, the handrail must have landed on the one of the blankets and struck one of the—*eggs*—objects beneath, making a huge dent that ruined the perfectly round surface. One edge of a dark brown blanket had fallen away, revealing a small section of a translucent pink sphere beneath.

"What the fuck is that?"

It wasn't a question, not really; more a statement, an incredulous utterance. Fear. Incomprehension.

Kent didn't know who said those words—they were

incredibly high-pitched, which suggested Baird, but they could have easily have been his own.

A frothy pink substance seemed to be spilling out of a ragged hole in the side of the orb, soaking the brown blanket that still covered most of it.

Then Kent heard the cracking sound again, and his eyes snapped away from the strange pink sphere and scanned the back wall. This time, it had sounded muffled, as if the culprit had burrowed beneath one of the thick brown blankets.

Tyler inexplicably took a shuffling step forward, and then another.

"Tyler!" Kent hissed.

He reached out for the boy, but with his hand still winding the crank furiously, he could only stretch a few inches. He missed the back of Tyler's sweatshirt by a hair.

"Tyler!" he hissed again, but either Tyler didn't hear him, or he simply chose to ignore his pleas.

Tyler took three more steps forward, and on his fourth step he was within reaching distance of the frothing pink orb.

"Tyler!"

It was Sergio this time.

"Get the fuck out of there! Jump up, and we'll grab you and pull you up."

But Tyler appeared as if he were in a trance, and continued to shuffle forward on his injured ankle, oblivious to their shouts. To Kent's horror, Tyler bent down, an

awkward half twist obviously meant to protect his injured ankle. But instead of touching the pink liquid or
the translucent sphere—thank God—he grabbed the
loose corner of the blanket instead. Then he hesitated.

Tyler, let's get the fuck out of here!

Kent's tears returned. His arm was burning, and he
could feel blisters beginning to form on his hand.

The blanket had an odd thickness to it, and Tyler's
fingers sunk into the material when he tightened his
grip. Without warning, the boy pulled the corner upward violently, but it didn't fly off like Kent expected.
Instead, it seemed to catch as if it were attached, fused to
the pink object beneath.

As Tyler held the blanket there, suspended in midair,
Kent caught a glimpse of the underside. It was smooth
and damp, but that wasn't what caused his heartrate to
double; even in the pale yellow glow from the bare bulb,
he made out a vast network of vessels embedded deep
within the blanket. Where the blanket still clung stub-
bornly to the round pink object, Kent could see the vessels migrate out of the smooth underside and *merge* with
the round surface.

Vessels. These are vessels and they are feeding it.

"It's like a fucking skin," Tyler whispered. "An animal skin."

He pulled again, and there was a sharp tearing noise
like separating Velcro, and Kent saw the blanket peel
away a few more inches from the top of the round
shape.

Egg. It looks like an egg. Only this was egg was broken—this egg was hatched. *The* palil *has hatched.*

Kent shook his head, unsure of where that word—
palil—had come from; he had never heard it before, and
had no idea what it meant. But, somehow, he thought it
fit.

Palil. The palil has hatched.

"Tyler, don't—" But once again his words caught in
his throat.

The cracking sound interrupted him, but this time it
wasn't rhythmic as it had been before, but several *cracks*
sounding in rapid succession.

Then he saw it.

It was just a shadow at first, a blur of darkness scamp-
ering on top of the blanket nearest the wall before it
scuttled toward where Tyler was standing. Except Tyler
was still inspecting the blanket—or *skin,* or whatever the
fuck it was—and he failed to take notice. Kent knew that
he should warn him, yell out, fucking *scream,* but he was
unable to do anything but turn the damn crank like
some sort of robot.

The shape moved fluidly across the top of the lumpy
blanket, managing the uneven surface with ease. It
stopped a few feet from Tyler, coming to an abrupt halt
directly in line with the dull glow from the light that
continued to struggle to penetrate the dust-filled air.

The creature was roughly the size of a small dinner
plate; a thick, milky white dinner plate like a newly

molted crab. And it did kind of look like a crab, although it *wasn't* a crab—it wasn't quite *right*. For one, the creature had six legs instead of eight, and each of the legs had several joints—*too* many knots of cartilage—at least four or five by Kent's count.

"Fucking stuck," Tyler grumbled as he tried to yank the blanket back once more.

The thing suddenly reared up—which was the only way Kent knew how to describe it—the many joints in those six legs articulating oddly, almost robotically. The revealed underside was a moist, opaque white, which at first Kent thought was featureless. But then the thing hissed, and he noticed a small, quarter-sized puckering orifice in the center of its mass. And inside this orifice, Kent caught a glimpse of row upon row of miniature teeth.

Staring at those rows of oscillating teeth, Kent knew that there was no way that both of them were getting out of the basement alive.

16.

"TYLER!" SOMEONE SHOUTED, BUT it was too late. When the boy finally looked up from the network of capillaries on the underside of what Kent was fairly certain now was a pelt or skin of some sort, the milky white thing had already dropped back down on all six of its legs. As he watched in horror, it lowered even further in time with the rhythmic cracking of its jointed appendages, each seeming to stiffen and lock into place.

"Tyler?" Kent whispered.

Before Tyler could answer, there was another crack, a louder, more defined sound, and the crab-like creature — the *palil* — suddenly flung itself through the air, covering the distance between it and Tyler in what could only be described as grace. In the blink of an eye, the thing landed square on the side and back of Tyler's shaved

head and the boy screamed. Almost immediately upon
impact, the articulated leg joints fanned out until the
thing was flush against the side of his head like a cap.
Then it seemed to lock into place, and Tyler screamed
again.

"What's going on?" Sergio yelled.

Kent couldn't tear his eyes away to look up, but he
thought that perhaps Tyler was too deep in the dark
room for them to see the *thing* that was latched onto his
head.

"Get it off me!" Tyler screamed, but his own hands
hung in midair at shoulder level, clearly indecisive.

Kent was still frozen, but he couldn't leave, couldn't
go to his friend, even if he wanted to; he had to keep
turning the crank. The thought of being immersed in
darkness with that *thing* was unbearable.

Tyler started to yell continuously now, a noise that re-
verberated off the brick walls of the basement like a
drumroll.

"Tyler? Kent?" Sergio cried from above. "What the
fuck is going on down there?"

Kent didn't answer, but even if he could've found the
words, he would have remained silent; he had no idea
what the *fuck* was happening.

Tyler was waving his hands above his head, moving
them in concentric circles, and with every rotation he got
closer and closer to thing that was pressed against his
shaved scalp.

"Kent?" he whispered, his eyes wet. "What the fuck is

it?"

Kent shook his head slowly, tears streaming from his own eyes.

"Please," Tyler pleaded, "get it off me."

There was a loud crunching sound and the crab suddenly contracted, and it was as if Tyler's skin—all of it, all of the skin covering his entire face and head—was *pulled* in the direction of the crab. He started to moan as his eyebrow and eyelids were pulled upward, his left nostril and the corner of his mouth extending unnaturally. As Kent watched, the boy's eyes began to roll back into his head.

"Get it off me," he blubbered between moans.

"What the fuck is going on down there? Get out of there!" Sergio screeched.

"I can't move!" Kent finally managed to blurt out, eyes still wide in horror. "I have to keep turning the fucking handle! Rip it off, Tyler!"

Although Tyler was still moaning, a long, undulating wail, his hands stopped whirring for a moment and they hovered just a few inches above the crab-like thing.

"Take it off!" Kent yelled, furiously cranking the handle. "Just pull the fucking thing off!"

Somewhere mixed with the buzzing electricity and whirring fan, he picked up the undertones of more cracking sounds, again muffled. It sounded like someone popping small packing bubbles under a blanket. There were more of these things under the animal skins, of that Kent had no doubt.

Tyler's hands finally came down on top of the creature, his fingers overlapping on its surface. For another moment he hesitated, a grimace forming on his face as he felt the strange texture beneath his palms. Then Kent saw Tyler's eyes roll forward, and his grasp of the thing tightened to the point that his knuckles went a stark white even in the dim yellow glow from the lightbulb.

"Pull, Tyler, pull!"

Tyler pulled. He pulled so hard that his face—his horribly stretched face—started to turn a deep red, bordering on purple. At first, nothing happened, but Tyler gritted his teeth and persisted, grunting as he tried to pry the crab from his head.

"Come over here," Kent shouted, still turning the handle. His arm and shoulder were screaming now, his muscles begging for him to stop.

Tyler, still pulling at the crab, took an awkward step toward Kent. The cracking sound, coming from somewhere behind his friend, intensified, but Kent barely noticed. His eyes were transfixed on the milky *palil* that seemed to have adhered to Tyler's head.

After another few steps, he passed within view of the boys above, and Kent heard a collective intake of breath. Kent used all of his willpower to avoid looking behind Tyler, to avoid focusing on the disturbing movements beneath the brown fur that flashed in his periphery.

When Tyler stumbled to within a foot of Kent, he finally got a good look at the thing, and immediately realized that it was not smooth as he had first thought. Instead, he noticed hundreds of tiny perforations speckling the otherwise hard surface that seemed to flutter every few seconds, the thin membrane surrounding the interior of each vibrating like a miniature blowhole.

The thing's legs were flattened against Tyler's head and face, one of them covering most of his left eye. And it had six knuckles and not four or five as Kent had first thought, each one a knot of tough cartilage-like tissue.

Tyler moaned again, and when his fingers tensed as he again tried to yank the thing off his head, Kent realized just how far his skin was stretched. There were small dots of blood forming at the corners of his left eyelid and nostril, and the skin in these places was so thin that it was bordering on translucent. Kent shuddered.

"Do something! Kent, fucking do something!" Sergio screamed, and something inside Kent broke.

At long last, Kent made a decision.

He reached out with his free hand and grabbed the thing's surface, trying to reach around the backside between Tyler's hands.

The *palil* was damp, cold, and hard. Every few seconds, the hundreds of tiny orifices fluttered, puffing cool air between Kent's fingers. The sensation made him gag—it was like holding a perforated crab, one that thrummed and vibrated like a hummingbird. Mustering all of his courage, he grasped the ridge separating the hard topside and leathery underside with his free hand and yanked it toward himself, trying to use the front edge as a lever.

Nothing. It didn't move at all.

He yanked again, and Tyler coordinated his efforts and pulled with him. This time, the crab-thing seemed to lift a bit; but instead of seeing dead space between the crab and Tyler's head, it took the skin with it.

A cluster of bloody spider webs splayed from the corner of Tyler's eye as his skin reached its elastic end.

"Get it off," Tyler pleaded, the tears spilling from his eye mixing with the blood, forming pink streaks that traced down his cheeks.

Kent could see deeper into his friend's eye socket than he had ever wanted to, and felt his gut revolt. It was all he could do to keep from letting go of the handle and vomiting.

"Tyler! Kent! What the fuck is going on?" Sergio screamed from above.

Kent ignored the shouts and Tyler's continuous moaning and tried to concentrate.

It was clear that the thing—the *palil*—wouldn't come off by pulling it unless it took Tyler's skin with it, which wasn't an option.

Kent's eyes flicked to the handle that his now numb arm cranked, and then to the debris around his feet from the collapsed staircase. He released his grip from the crab.

"What're you doing?" Tyler moaned. "Don't let go! Keep pulling!"

Kent ignored his friend; he had made up his mind.

The only thing that made sense was to smash the *palil*;
letting go of the handle and smash the hissing fucker in
the darkness. A dangerous proposition, no less, as if he
missed the thing then he could very well brain Tyler.

His eyes darted to the blood that now spilled from the
network of splits in Tyler's stretched face.

No other option.

To his left, just three or four feet from him, was what
looked like half of a stair tread that had smashed in such
a way that one end was tapered. Eyeing the splintered
end, he thought he might be able to grip it.

"Go get help!" he screamed over Tyler's moans and
the increasingly loud cracking sound from beneath the
fur pelts. "Sergio, Baird, go get some fucking help!"

"I'm not goin—"

"Go get some fucking help!" Kent screamed hysteri-
cally.

He took one last look at Tyler's stretched face, the
boy's fluttering eyelids, his hands still clutching the *palil*,
rhythmically pulling the thing so that it looked like his
face was pulsating, and Kent made up his mind.

Without hesitating, Kent stopped spinning the handle
and leaned far to his left, feeling for the wood as the
light blinked out almost immediately. He nearly ca-
reened over onto his side, his body confused by the fact
that his arm was no longer spinning around in a rapid
circle. Righting himself, Kent reached into the darkness,
his outstretched fingers trying to grasp the broken stair,
all the while trying not to stray far from the hand crank.

His heart skipped a beat when his groping hand didn't immediately find the wood. His fingers desperately clawed at the dirt floor, so much of it collecting beneath his nails that he nearly cried out.

A crack—one of those synovial pops—sounded so close to him that he almost pissed himself.

No! Please, no!

But then his fingers scraped across the familiar surface of worn wood, and he immediately grabbed the narrow end of the stair. Having found the object, he managed to orient himself and scrambled back to his feet before moving directly to his right.

Amazingly, his hand found the handle of the crank generator almost immediately, and although every muscle on his right side protested—his shoulder, bicep, and back—he forced himself to spin it again.

In the thirty or so seconds that had passed since the lights had gone off, things had changed. And not for the better.

Tyler must have staggered backward in the darkness, as he was now a few feet closer to the fur-covered eggs, and his eyes had completely rolled back into his head so that only the whites were visible. The chitinous, cracking creature—the *cracker*— seemed unchanged; it was still fused to Tyler's shaved head, the tiny blowholes still fluttering every few seconds. Kent inspected it closely for a second, trying to figure out if it had eyes or some other sensitive organ that he might be able to poke with the sharp end of the piece of wood instead of striking it.

He found nothing; it was just a symmetrical, flattened disc with six knobby legs.

A particularly low moan spewed from Tyler's open mouth, and his knees buckled. It was clear that he only had a moment or two before Tyler collapsed, passed out, or succumbed to whatever the thing was doing to him.

Grip it and rip it.

He heard muffled voices from above and more cracking from behind Tyler, but he drowned out these distractions and readied himself.

Despite only using one hand, the broken stair's arced descent was violent and deliberate. It struck the top of the hard crab shell studded with the hundreds of tiny holes, and Kent heard a new sound: a hollow *thunk* that sounded like a boulder being dropped into a lake.

Then his entire left side erupted in vibrations.

17.

IT WAS A MISTAKE; all of it was a mistake.

Leaving the confines of their tents; drinking the bottle of vodka; coming to this abandoned Estate and playing *Ba di ba*. It was a mistake to stop pulling the cracker, it was a mistake telling Baird and Sergio to leave, and it was a mistake to try to smash the cracker with the broken wooden step. Mistakes, all of them.

The shell did not fracture like Kent had expected, despite the speed of his strike and the sound that it made when the blow landed. But it didn't go unnoticed, either; instead, the thing started to move.

At first, the legs that had been flattened against Tyler's skull started to curl up, bending at the many joints in a coordinated, almost hypnotic, manner. Then the cracker seemed to *disengage* from Tyler's skin, although judging by the way the boy's moans continued unabated, this offered him little relief.

As the legs retracted, the suction from the tiny, tooth-filled orifice seemed to lessen and the tear marks on Tyler's skin seemed to relax. Kent's stomach did another barrel roll. The skin on the boy's face was loose—*too loose*—and it seemed to have disconnected from the muscle and sinew beneath, the sagging flesh hanging over his left eye socket like a limp sail on a windless day. It was as if Tyler had developed some sort of palsy or affect; the whole left side of his face dropped dramatically. What made it worse was that his eye hole didn't line up perfectly anymore; Kent couldn't make out the white part of his eye beneath the sagging upper lid, while the lower hung too low, revealing a wet red tangle of muscle.

Kent almost swung the piece of wood again, thinking that the cracker might be more vulnerable now that it had *detached*, but before he had a chance to react, the thing seemed to prop itself up on those six heavily jointed legs like a tripod. The *palil* paused once it reached its apex, stretching to about eight or ten inches above Tyler's head, and Kent caught a glimpse of the ragged hole in Tyler's skin where it had been affixed. If it had had recognizable eyes, Kent would have guessed it was staring at him.

Still turning the handle like a madman, Kent finally allowed himself a shallow breath, but remained otherwise still. He was mesmerized by the way the thing seemed to flutter every few seconds as air was forced through those tiny holes all at once.

I should hit it again — swipe it off his head.

But Kent did nothing — he couldn't make up his mind. Instead, he watched helplessly as the thing cracked once — a hard, resounding *snap* — its legs articulating beneath its body at alarming speed, forming a single, almost drill-like appendage.

What happened next made Kent piss himself.

The *palil* seemed to dive into the ragged hole it had made in Tyler's skin, dissecting what little sinewy connections remained as it burrowed *beneath* the boy's flesh. Then, somehow, inexplicably, the thing managed to flip over in the confined pace, the small, anus-like orifice wriggling back and forth until it centered on the hole in his skin, the multitude of tiny teeth now exposed to the outside world.

Tyler staggered backwards, but his ungainly movements did nothing to stop the cracker's progress. The legs slowly and methodically articulated the other way — double-jointed, it appeared — so that once again they were completely flat against his head, only this time they were beneath his skin. It looked like six sausages pressed beneath a thin layer of uncooked filo pastry; six horrific Beef Wellingtons ready to go into the oven.

Like a madman, and fearing that he was indeed going mad, Kent continued to spin the crank, his body in full automation mode now, the warmth spreading from his crotch not even registering.

It was odd how, what with Tyler's stretched skin and the thing now burrowed beneath, the holes—the eyes, the mouth—almost seemed to line up again.

Almost perfect, Kent thought, his head spinning.

Except, of course, it wasn't perfect; there was a knobby protrusion that was buried at his temple like a shallow, upside-down bowl.

At the same moment that Tyler's body went limp, Kent heard a chorus of other cracks—groups of six, all the same cadence.

Crack. Crack. Crack. Crack. Crack. Crack.

More movement caught his eye, and for the first time in what seemed like an eternity, Kent managed to look away from his boyhood friend. There, perched on top of the now ragged brown, grey, and black furs were about a half dozen crackers, all poised, all of their bodies lowering—crouching—in unison as each of their horrible six legs snapped into place.

The timing was nearly perfect: just as Tyler fell backward into the mass of eggs and skins, the crackers sprang, two of them landing and immediately suctioning to his head while the others landed on his exposed hands and neck.

Unlike the first cracker, these ones took no time burrowing into and underneath the boy's skin.

Kent heard Tyler utter one final moan before his body sunk into the animal skins, a bubbling sound and a gassy release spewing forth as his body was quickly coated in an obscene frothy bath.

Kent could take it no longer. His turned to the hole in the ceiling, at what had once been the stairwell entrance — the trapdoor. Then, without thinking, he let go of the crank handle and bolted toward the opening just as the light faded and he was once again immersed in blackness.

18.

KENT HAD NO IDEA how he had managed to get out of the basement, let alone how he had sprinted his way across the charred foyer, through the open doorway, and into the pitch black night. The burning scrapes on his palms and forearms suggested that he had somehow leapt from and scrambled out of the basement, but he couldn't even remember making the decision to leave. He was sweating profusely as he ran, his right arm now completely numb, his inner thighs chafing from the salt left behind by his urine.

But he ran onward, these sensations an afterthought to the horror he had just experienced.

He had no obvious destination; he only knew that he had to get as far away from the house as possible—as far away from those *things* as possible. But no matter how fast he ran, or how loud the blood rushing in his ears or the wheezy gasps from his own spit-covered lips as his lungs desperately tried to soak up oxygen, he heard that snapping sound.

Crack.

Crack.

Crack

Crack.

Crack.

Crack.

Kent heard those cracks, like distinct knuckles, each with their own identical synovial bubble being popped.

No matter how fast Kent ran, he heard the *palil*, the *crackers*.

Epilogue

SILENCE.

Sheriff Paul White was aware of his breathing, but he couldn't hear it. The only thing he heard were the boy's words repeating over and over in his mind like a strange mantra.

I have no idea how I got out…

And it was the boy's choice of words, the strange ones, the ones that were not English.

The ones that he had never heard before, but somehow sounded *familiar* to him.

Palil.

It was a word that should have meant nothing to him, but somehow it did. Somehow that word epitomized the

shit that went down at the Wharfburn Estate both this
time and six years ago during the blizzard.

The sheriff opened his mouth to say something, but
he found that his throat was too dry to squeeze the
words out. Instead, he reached across the table and
grabbed the half-full glass of water from the boy and
took a sip.

Then he cleared his throat and at long last addressed
the two people across from him.

"Kent, I want to thank you for coming down here, for
telling me what happened."

It had been a fantastical story, one that seemed impossible.

But the boy's recounting had been flawless, down to
the very minute details.

Gregory Griddle nodded.

"What happens now, Sheriff?"

The sheriff took a moment to contemplate this.

What do I do next?

"Sheriff?"

Paul looked from the man back to the boy with the
red face. Kent turned to his father, and the man wrapped
his arms around his son, comforting him.

Despite what the sheriff believed, the boy's father believed all of his son's tale.

"I think—" The sheriff cleared his throat again. "I
think there is someone else I need to talk to."

Gregory nodded.

"What about us? What do we do now?"

"You guys go home and get some rest."

Gregory's expression remained blank, vacant.

Rest? He berated himself for the suggestion. There was no way these two were going to be able to sleep. Not after…

He turned to Kent, whose face was now completely buried in his father's armpit.

After what the boy had seen, he doubted that rest was something that Kent could even comprehend at this point—and probably not for a long, long time.

"Try," the sheriff reiterated, doing his best not to placate. "I have someone to talk to, and I'm sure that he will want to speak to you too."

I have someone who I need to talk to, someone who was also inside the Wharfburn Estate, Paul wished he could say. *Someone who might be able to make sense of all of this.*

"But we are going to find your friend, Kent," he continued.

Someone who has their own secrets, ones that rival the dark tale that you just uttered, Kent.

Gregory leaned toward his son and kissed him on his forehead. Then he nodded to the sheriff.

"Please, anything we can do to help."

The man stood and they shook hands.

"I mean that. Anything."

The sheriff nodded.

Someone who likely has as much trouble sleeping at night as you will, Kent. I need to find the boy; I need to find Tyler Wandry.

And Bradley Coggins can help, no matter his state of mind.

End

AUTHOR'S NOTE

If you liked this novella, please leave a review where you bought it. Reviews help readers like you find similar books that they might enjoy.

The *Insatiable Series* continues with **Flesh** (Insatiable Book 3), available November, 2015.

Now for a sneak preview, enjoy the first three chapters of **Flesh**...

FLESH

Insatiable Series
Book 3

PROLOGUE

SWEAT BEADED ON THE BRICKS, tiny droplets of perspiration in the form of condensed humidity. It was unbearably hot in the basement, and the air was thick, housing equal parts dust and water.

A hand suddenly reached out of the hole in the floor, the long, thin fingers stretching skyward. Bright sunlight from the open doorway splayed between the digits. As the arm continued to stretch upward, a thin forearm cleared the opening, followed by the inner side of a knobby elbow. Without warning, the arm came down on the hardwood, the fingers splaying out, desperately seeking purchase on the dusty floor.

There was a grunt, and then another hand appeared, only this one was heavy, almost *bulbous*, the fingers not clearly discernable from each other, each blending together like a mitten. When it landed on the floor above, it did so with an ungainly thud.

The hands and arms tensed, and a figure rose clumsily out of the basement, collapsing onto the floor and rolling onto its back with another series of grunts.

Grey shafts of light continued to penetrate the abandoned Estate, slipping through tiny cracks and holes in the boards that covered the windows. A large flood of light spilled through the open front door, reflecting off the dust motes that fluttered in the newly disturbed air. *Hot. Too hot.*

The naked figure flipped onto its front and then labored to its feet, remaining hunched at the waist, hiding its upper half from the offensive sunlight. The thing's mottled flesh was covered in sweat, but unlike the bricks in the basement below, the beads were not individual entities, but had coalesced into a sheen that covered the entire surface of its entire body. With several desperate, lurching strides, it made its way to the back of the house, creeping its way along the cabinets that lined the kitchen, then strafed the wall as it tried to stay out of the direct sunlight.

The back of the house had been boarded up, but it managed to pry these rotten planks off without much effort, despite having to resort to using its only good hand.

A sigh escaped the thing as it exited the house and entered the still cool and dewy morning air, the shadow provided by the peaked roof of the Estate protecting the area from the sun's onslaught for the time being.

It wouldn't last long.

The shambling mass avoided the large swimming pool, its meandering gait taking it wide to avoid an unfortunate misstep. When its feet left the cobblestones and touched the cool grass, another wave of relief washed over it, culminating in a veritable shudder that made its progress look robotic, as if filmed at a low framerate.

At the back of the property was a culvert, an ancient cement tunnel that led beneath a small two-lane road.

The figure collapsed in the shady interior of the tunnel, not bothering to push aside the network of spider webs or detritus that lined the interior of the forgotten passage.

Cool; the cement was cool, and was a welcome relief to his overheating face and stomach.

As it shut its eyes, the skin on its naked back just above the left shoulder blade suddenly began to stretch, pushing the already extended membrane to its maximum. An outline became apparent beneath the blistering white skin, a protruding oval about six inches across; an oval with six knobby, articulated limbs.

The skin on the figure's back puckered, then tore. A groan escaped its chapped lips, but it wasn't a manifestation of pain; rather, sweet relief washed over it as the tension from its stretched skin was momentarily relieved. A warm wetness spread from the spot on its back from where the cracker had budded, a wetness that could only be one thing: blood.

It didn't matter.

What mattered was the cool cement on its stomach; what mattered was the relief from its stretched skin.

The individual points of the cracker's appendages, all six of them, slowly pressed into its skin, making small indentations just outside of the wound. A moment later, the hole that it had erupted from slowly began to become obscured, a layer of milky white skin pushing up to the surface. Another few seconds and the ragged, bloody hole was completely replaced by this new layer of thin white flesh.

A cracking sound echoed off of the undulating walls of the culvert; six cracks, all the same cadence.

Crack. Crack. Crack. Crack. Crack. Crack.

Then the cracker was gone, leaving what was once a boy lying face down on his stomach, alone, his skin beginning to stretch again, the outline of another cracker slowly becoming visible beneath the surface.

PART I – BUDDING

1.

THE MAN WITH THE bushy red beard raised his head from his lap and looked around.

The bathroom was filthy, the walls—which might have once been white, or in the very least eggshell— were now so streaked with dirty grey smudges that they seemed to meld into an obscene background color. There was the usual graffiti, phone numbers etched with red pens and promises of sexual acts of the kind that might have once made him blush. There were the ubiquitous swastikas, drops of blood, promises of castration, and various curses, each less intelligible than the last. But none of these were of interest to him.

The slurping sound from between his legs stopped for a moment, and he turned his gaze downward.

A pair of bright green eyes stared up at him, expectant.

"Don't stop," he instructed the woman.

The woman nodded and then buried her head in his lap once more.

No, none of the graffiti bothered him, except for one.

He leaned forward, and the woman kneeling on the floor between his legs shifted to accommodate his movements. Her pace quickened, clearly misinterpreting his gesture. On the left wall of the bathroom stall was a picture of a large shape, something akin to a morbidly obese man, crudely drawn with a green crayon. It was a generally featureless mass, except for two vertical lines in yellow at the center of its head. Beneath the shape were two words: *Oot'-keban*.

The man's breath caught in his throat and he blinked hard, not believing what he was seeing. He leaned forward further, reaching out with his hand to wipe some of the grime away.

The woman protested, again pulling her head up, but this time, instead of indicating for her to continue, he used his other hand to push her head to one side.

She grumbled something but he ignored her, moving closer still to the crudely drawn shape. When his eyes focused in the dim light, a sigh escaped him. It wasn't a person after all, just a green circle. And what he had first thought were yellow eyes were just a row of lights that went all the way around the shape. The words beneath the space ship weren't *Oot'-keban*, either, but *Art Cabin*.

Spaceship. Just a fucking alien spaceship.

He slumped back onto the top of the toilet seat, his heartrate finally returning to normal. The woman between his legs set about returning to her business, but any semblance of *mood* in the grimy stall was gone.

"Naw," he grumbled, using the palm of his hand to push her forehead away again.

She looked up at him, her mouth open, incredulous. She had a shock of white-blonde hair pulled back in a tight ponytail, which was obviously meant to serve two purposes: the color was supposed to make her look younger, and the tight ponytail was meant to stretch out her skin, smooth some of the wrinkles.

Both attempts failed; this was a woman who had been around the block, a fact that was reflected in her tired face.

"What you mean, 'No'?"

She smacked a piece of bubble gum loudly and pushed a stray strand of white hair from her face.

The man began to stand.

"I mean, 'no' —not in the mood anymore." His words were languid, apathetic.

She smacked the gum several more times before slowly pulling herself to her feet.

"Well, you're still paying me," she informed him, her mouth tight. Her hands smoothed and lowered the short jean skirt that had ridden up when she had squatted.

He looked away, pushing the stall door open behind her. The woman stepped backward.

"Fine," he said absently, hiking up his own jeans.

He tucked himself back in and then zipped up his jeans. Then he reached into his wallet and pulled out a fifty. He hadn't even put his wallet back into his back pocket before her manicured hand reached out and snatched the bill from him.

Then she blew a large pink bubble and turned away, stepping out of the stall and going over to the large, cracked mirror above a porcelain sink.

"Thanks," she said between chews.

"Whatever," he grumbled.

The man stretched his back, then watched as the prostitute leaned close to the mirror and opened her mouth wide, using one of her fingers to wipe away smeared lipstick from the corner of her lips.

As the man left the stall and made his way toward the door leading back to the bar, the woman turned to him again.

"There are pills for that, you know," she said, her expression tight.

"Pills? For what?"

The woman's large green eyes drifted down his body and her gaze lingered on his crotch.

The man laughed.

"It's not me, baby, it's you," he said, and then laughed again at the confused look that fell on her pale face.

The palm of his hand struck the back of the door and pushed it open an inch. Music and loud voices articulated their way through the opening. Now it was his turn to stop and face her.

"Anyways," he continued, the smile still plastered on his bearded face, "that was my last fifty. Care to buy a fella a drink?"

2.

AN ARM SLOWLY SNAKED its way around her neck, the fingers dissecting her chin that had been driven protectively her chest. The girl grunted, trying to shake the man's body from her back, but he was too heavy, his center of gravity too high up on her shoulders. On her elbows and knees, she crouched herself into a tight ball, trying to build up as much potential energy as possible, conserving her strength for one final explosive move.

Just as her assailant's fingers reached his bicep on the other side of her neck, but before he could lock in the chokehold, the girl exploded, turning her head quickly into the choke while at the same time sliding one of her legs flat. The spontaneity and precision of the movement caught the man off guard, and in one smooth motion, she turned her body over, flipping her assailant onto his back.

Breathing heavily, she found herself on top of the man, sitting on his chest, staring down at his tense face, his eyes staring up at her in surprise.

But this man was a brown belt, and his surprise was only temporary.

The man bucked her unexpectedly, and she, being at least thirty pounds lighter, became airborne, her body launched up toward his head. Her first instinct was to come down on his head with her elbows, driving his head into the mat beneath them, but she fought this urge and attempted instead to land gracefully.

In the end, her intentions were irrelevant, as immediately after he bucked her, the man slid down her body, grabbing ahold of her right ankle as he passed. In one smooth transition, he hooked her heel under his arm and gave her leg a yank, pulling her onto her back for the second time in the last forty seconds.

"Fuck," she swore, momentarily dazed when the back of her head made contact with the ground.

This time, the man didn't make the mistake of slowly locking in his hold; this time, his grip was fast and furious, and before she knew it, her ankle was wrenched completely sideways, and with one of the man's legs laced across her chest, she found herself unable to roll out of the heel-hook.

She grunted and tried to reach for the man's leg, to defend against the ankle lock by putting him into one of her own, but he twisted his legs away from her. Her fingers reached across the mat, desperate now, the pressure building in her quad, trying to seek out any part of the man's body that she might be able to attack.

Nothing—her desperate fingers found no purchase.

The man grunted and increased the pressure on her ankle.

"Tap," he demanded. He yanked her foot again, turning it so far that it was almost perpendicular. "Tap." The girl shifted her hips, trying to buck him as he had done to her in an attempt to get him to loosen his grip so that she might pull her leg out from beneath his armpit and yank herself to her feet.

It was no use. His grip was solid, unbreakable.

"Tap," he repeated a third time. He twisted her ankle beyond ninety degrees as he spoke, emphasizing his words.

Now it was her turn to do something unexpected. Instead of trying to turn into the hold and protect her ankle, she turned against it. This only helped tighten the man's grip, as her foot became even more anchored in his armpit. This move, a seemingly basic mistake, actually surprised the man, and she felt his grip loosen for a moment. Yet she did not alter course and try to get out of the hold; she had tried that already and knew it wouldn't work. Besides, as before, the man's surprise was short-lived, and he quickly clamped his arms down, doubling the pressure on her ankle.

With a grunt of her own, she twisted her hips as hard as she could, and an audible pop filled the gym. This time, the man's surprise was so great that he completely let go of her ankle, his eyes bulging from his sockets in horror. At this point, however, it didn't matter—she was already out.

"What the fuck?" The man's face twisted as the girl's leg suddenly came free just above the knee and he was stuck holding nothing but a prosthetic limb.

The girl used this prolonged surprise to her advantage, and quickly scrambled on top of the man's chest. Then, staring into his wide eyes, she brought her right elbow down in a high arc. She heard the man's nose crunch, and then felt the unmistakable warm sensation of blood on her forearm.

"Corina!" someone shouted from off to her right.

She ignored the cry, and raised her arm to deliver another crushing blow when a meaty hand grabbed her forearm from behind.

"Corina!" The man's breath reeked of stale coffee, a scent that strangely brought her around.

Her entire body went limp, and she allowed herself to be pulled off. The man's hands immediately went to his broken nose, his eyes watering.

"What the fuck, Corina?" he said, his voice coming out nasally and high-pitched.

Corina turned her large hazel eyes to the floor, immediately ashamed of what she had done. The man that she had brutally elbowed quickly scampered to his feet, grabbing the heel of her prosthetic leg and tossing it like a loose helicopter blade into the corner of the room.

"Fucking bitch," he muttered, staring at the blood that filled his palm.

"Take a walk, Teddy. Go get cleaned up," said the man who'd grabbed Corina's arm.

The man with the broken nose waved the old man away, but he said nothing further and turned his back to both of them.

Corina, eyes still downcast, pulled away from the now loose grip on her forearm, turning her foot sideways to balance herself on one leg. Then she turned and looked at the man who had prevented her from delivering what would have probably been at least another half dozen blows.

There was no humor in the man's heavily lined face. His eyes were a rich blue, and they focused on her intently, trying to figure out if she had calmed down. Above his eyes was a thick thatch of eyebrows that were knitted tightly, the inner corners nearly touching in a Scorsese sort of way. The man—who Corina assumed was in his late sixties or early seventies, although she had never asked him directly—had short grey hair cropped close to his skull. Despite his age, the man's grip had been tight, and so was the rest of him. Sure, like everyone his age his skin had lost some of its elasticity, and in a few key places it sagged a bit—beneath his chin, on the underside of his wrists, around his knees—but he would never be mistaken as one of the out-of-shape bingo players from down the hall. No, years of jiu jitsu and boxing training had turned his physique into a rock—a rock with a light layer of moss covering the surface.

"I'm sorry," Corina whispered, looking away from her mentor's face. For nearly five years she had been coming here, turning his dojo into her own personal shrink to work out her problems.

Her attention was drawn to the bloody smear on the underside of her forearm. Obviously, it would take more than physical activities, irrespective of how violent, to exorcise her demons.

The man's voice matched his physique; hard and gravelly.

"Sorry's not going to cut it this time, Corina," Mr. Gillespie said.

Her eyes snapped up.

Not gonna cut it?

This wasn't the first time that someone she had been rolling with had ended up bloody—all the other times Mr. Gillespie had just told her to shower up.

But none of those partners had been Teddy Manfred, the son of the man that owned the building that Mr. Gillespie leased to run the dojo.

Corina shook her head slowly, the sweaty strips of short brown hair clinging uncomfortably to her cheeks and scalp.

"I need this," she pleaded. "Please, Mr—"

He cut her off.

"Corina, you broke Teddy's nose." His voice softened. "You know what he could to this place."

Corina felt tears welling in her eyes. This was all she had—he couldn't take this away from her.

"Please," she begged.

Something in the old man's face broke, and his hard expression became flaccid. He brought a hand to the heavy lines around his mouth and rubbed them.

"Look, Corina, just take some time off and I'll talk to Teddy. But you need some real help, and I—this place—can't give it to you anymore."

"How much time is 'some'?" she asked, ignoring the last comment.

Mr. Gillespie's blue eyes focused on hers.

"A month," he said. "Two would be better, but a month will do. Will give me some time to smooth things over with Teddy and his dad. You know Teddy—he's a fucking prima donna, thinks he's UFC champion or something." He paused, then repeated, "A month."

Corina nodded. She would go mad without the gym for a month, but knew that she was getting off easy—besides, she knew that no matter how much Mr. Gillespie cared for her, he was not a man to go back on a decision once it had been made.

The man returned her nod and walked to the corner of the room and collected her prosthetic leg. He handed it to her, and Corina locked it into place. She opened her mouth to say something, but then closed it again. There was no more to be said.

Instead, she headed to the change room in silence.

A month. An entire month without the gym.

"Fuck."

3.

IT WASN'T THE MAN'S dark skin, or the fact that he
was six-foot-four and two hundred and sixty pounds of
mostly muscle in a place that was populated by fat white
men with burgeoning bellies, long grey beards, and tat-
toos marking most of their exposed pale flesh that made
him stand out. No, it was something as simple as his
shirt; not the *shirt* itself, as this was nothing more than a
beige button-down with short sleeves. Rather, it was
what was on his shirt: the patch on his triceps just before
the bottom of the sleeve, the one that read 'Askergan
County PD'. And, more specifically, it was the gold star
on his chest that read: SHERIFF. Sticking out like a sore
thumb in this place was an understatement.

But there was one man in the bar that didn't lean back
and take notice, and that was the man with the red

bushy beard and the crooked teeth that had emerged from the bathroom. Following only a few seconds after a pale woman with a blonde ponytail and jean skirt that was barely long enough to cover her ass cheeks, the man walked across the room, aware of but not acknowledging the sheriff who sat alone at the bar. He took the seat right next to the muscular police officer.

"Whiskey," the sheriff demanded, and the barkeep, a young man with jet black hair that was shaved on the sides but with a healthy crop on top, just stared at him.

The sheriff cleared his throat.

"Whiskey," he asked again.

The bartender sneered but obliged, turning his back to the sheriff and reaching for the lowest bottle on the glass shelf. "And get one for my friend here, too."

A moment later, the bartender turned back around with two rock glasses, one in each hand, the bottoms coated with a golden brown liquid. It was barely enough whiskey to cover the bottom, let alone a full ounce.

This didn't seem to bother the sheriff, and he downed it in one go. He twisted the glass back and forth in his meaty black hand.

"Another," he demanded, and the skinny bartender reluctantly took the glass from him.

"Do you like trivia?" the sheriff asked, turning to the man beside him.

The man with the red beard didn't respond.

"Well I do," the sheriff continued. "I have a few favorites, too. Wanna hear them?"

Again, the man to his left said nothing.

The sheriff continued, unfazed.

"Who is the only man in NHL history to score two overtime goals in one game?" the sheriff asked.

The man with the red beard cleared his throat.

"Chris Campoli," he said. Then he brought his own thimble of drink to his mouth and swallowed.

The sheriff smiled. This time, when the bartender turned with another glass of whiskey, the sheriff took a small sip and put the glass down on the bar instead of drinking it all at once. The barkeep turned back to the shelf and began drying some pint glasses, doing a terrible job of pretending he wasn't eavesdropping.

"How about this?" the sheriff continued, this time keeping his eyes straight ahead, focusing on the mirror on the wall behind the bartender "Who has the most three-on-five short-handed goals?"

The man with the red beard smirked; he couldn't help it. This was too easy.

"Mike Richards."

Again, the sheriff laughed.

"Good, good. But now—"

The sheriff hesitated. A flicker of movement in the mirror caught his eye. Two men were approaching them from behind, two large men wearing jeans and leather vests—straight out of the eighties. Following close behind was the blonde with the ponytail and red lipstick that had come out of the bathroom right before the man with the red beard.

The sheriff swiveled in his chair to face the men that approached.

The larger of the two men, an oaf who was nearly as big as the sheriff himself, stepped in front of him and pointed his pudgy finger aggressively.

"You're not welcome here."

The sheriff, unfazed, smiled, revealing a row of perfectly white teeth.

"You must have me mistaken for someone else," he said. Then he puffed his considerable chest and brought his own finger to the star on his vest, tapping it several times. "The name is Sheriff; Sheriff Paul White."

The biker sneered.

"This ain't Askergan. You're out of your jurisdiction."

Again, the other biker snorted.

"DICK-tion."

Sheriff White rolled his eyes.

The biker took offense to this and took another aggressive step forward, closing the distance between himself and the sheriff to under three feet. When he extended his finger again, the sheriff's face suddenly changed—his smile disappeared, hiding those brilliant white teeth behind his thick lips, and his hazel eyes went cold.

The movements were quick for such a big man; not lightning quick, but much faster than either of the bikers could have anticipated.

The sheriff's hand shot out and he grabbed the man's outstretched finger, yanking it hard to one side, snapping the bone just beyond the first knuckle. The biker cried out, and as he instinctively turned to look at his hand, the sheriff reared back and drove his massive fist directly into the man's face.

The biker never saw the blow coming and stumbled backward, taking the girl down with him as he collapsed on top of a round table. The table broke under his immense weight, smashing several pint glasses and spraying the stunned occupants with frothing liquid and glass fragments.

"What the *fuck*?!" the other biker shouted, his eyes darting from his fallen friend and the girl and then back at the sheriff. "You *fuck*!" He took a step forward.

During the altercation, the man with the bushy red beard had slipped off the stool and now, as the sheriff

readied himself, his right leg going forward, his fists
raised up in front of his face, the man casually took one
step to his right. The biker took another step forward,
and that was when the man with the red beard delivered
a vicious kick squarely to the side of the biker's knee.
The blow had been timed perfectly, and the biker's forward progress was immediately halted, a cry escaping
his lips.

Both of his hands immediately went his knee as he ca-
reened sideways, hopping on his other foot, trying desperately not to fall.

He lost the battle.

Another table was broken and more beer was spilled.

"Yeah, I think we better go," the man with the red
beard said. The shock was beginning to wear off, and the
men that had been sitting around the first smashed table
now helped the biker with the broken finger to his feet.

The sheriff nodded.

"Like, right now!" the man said.

The other half dozen men in the bar were standing
now, inspecting their beer-soaked clothes. The man with
the torn knee was still wailing on the ground, but they
stepped around him, not taking heed.

"Go!" the man with the red beard suddenly shouted,
and the sheriff, on cue, quickly turned and ran to the
door.

The other man followed.

The sheriff scrambled to get the car door to his cruiser
unlocked as the door to the bar banged open behind
them.

The man with the red beard turned back to the bar,
just as the sheriff opened his door and jumped into the
driver seat.

"You *motherfucker!*"

It was the man that Sheriff White had punched, his head tilted to one side, his uninjured hand probing his already swelling jaw. He turned his head to one side and spat a glob of blood onto the tarmac. The man with the red beard thought he saw a flash of white in the red splotch—a tooth, perhaps.

"Get in!" the sheriff yelled, and the man quickly obliged.

The sheriff peeled out of the parking lot, his squealing tires leaving the bikers in a cloud of dust and a trail of burnt rubber.

Thankfully, they were only about a dozen miles outside of Askergan, and despite the bikers' obvious fury, the sheriff knew that they wouldn't dare follow. And if they did, well, things would be very different on his turf.

After a minute or so, the sheriff's adrenaline drained and his heartrate returned to normal. He turned to his passenger.

"Classy joint you got there."

The man smirked, keeping his eyes straight ahead.

"Yeah, you fit right in," he replied.

The sheriff grunted. It had been almost five years since he had seen his friend, and despite his appearance—the horrible red beard, the greasy, shoulder-length brown hair—and his choice of drinking establishment, he could tell that not much had changed.

"Let's get you cleaned up, Coggins. Askergan needs you; Askergan needs the good boys again."

Andrew Coggins' smile faded, and he kept his eyes trained on the road ahead.

The good boys—Askergan needs the good boys.

Coggins, still silent, eyes focused ahead, reached up and flicked on the cherries.

Flesh, Book 3 in the Insatiable Series, is now available!

Order your copy today!

31173133R00119

Made in the USA
Middletown, DE
20 April 2016